Praise for the work of Sandra Steffen

"Steffen is one of those authors whose characters and
their emotions ring true, which makes each book a
heartfelt treat."
—*Romantic Times BOOKreviews*

"Steffen's characters are thoroughly and thoughtfully
conceived...the charm of this tale lies in her lovely
portrayal of complex family relationships."
—*Publishers Weekly* on *The Cottage*

"Sandra Steffen is a veritable master at creating characters.
On a scale of 1–10, a 15!"
—*ReaderToReader.com*

"Steffen knows exactly how hard to tug on readers'
heart-strings for maximum effect."
—*Booklist*

"A powerfully riveting story that pulls the reader in from
page one and doesn't stop...one of the most original plots
I've ever seen...flawless characterization."
—*Romance Reviews Today* on *Come Summer*

Sandra Steffen

Slightly Psychic isn't Sandra Steffen's first venture into tales about unexplainable psychic phenomena. *Child of Her Dreams*, one of her earliest novels (about a woman who is clairvoyant), won the 1994 National Reader's Choice award. Since then more than thirty-five of Sandra's novels have graced bookshelves in the United States and a dozen foreign countries. When she isn't writing, she's either thinking about writing or honing her slightly psychic abilities on her ever-growing circle of friends and family.

SANDRA STEFFEN
SLIGHTLY PSYCHIC

SLIGHTLY PSYCHIC

copyright © 2007 by Sandra E. Steffen

isbn-13:978-0-373-88125-3

isbn-10:   0-373-88125-8

All rights reserved. Except for use in any review, the reproduction
or utilization of this work in whole or in part in any form by any
electronic, mechanical or other means, now known or hereafter
invented, including xerography, photocopying and recording, or in
any information storage or retrieval system, is forbidden without the
written permission of the publisher, Harlequin Enterprises Limited,
225 Duncan Mill Road, Don Mills, Ontario, Canada M3B 3K9.

All characters in this book have no existence outside the imagination
of the author and have no relation whatsoever to anyone bearing the
same name or names. They are not even distantly inspired by any
individual known or unknown to the author, and all incidents are
pure invention.

This edition published by arrangement with Harlequin Books S.A.

® and TM are trademarks of the publisher. Trademarks indicated with
® are registered in the United States Patent and Trademark Office, the
Canadian Trade Marks Office and in other countries.

TheNextNovel.com

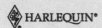 HARLEQUIN®

PRINTED IN U.S.A.

If you purchased this book without a cover you should be aware that
this book is stolen property. It was reported as "unsold and destroyed" to
the publisher, and neither the author nor the publisher has received any
payment for this "stripped book."

From the Author

Dear Reader,

I've just filled three hundred pages, and now, when I'm all out of words, I wish for a few more to tell you how pleased I am to be able to entertain you with my newest creation, *Slightly Psychic*. Goodness, I have *goose bumps!*

Partway into telling this story, I almost had to change the title to *Slightly Superstitious*. First my computer had a motherboard problem (oh, the angst!), then a few weeks ago it shut down and refused to restart. It seems the fan fell off inside. Since I've never thrown salt over my shoulder and my cat is black and brings me nothing but joy, I'm sticking with my original title. After all, we make our own luck... but all women (and some men) become *Slightly Psychic* eventually. I have a hunch you already knew that.

I'm off to buy a new computer so I'm ready when the inspiration for my next novel washes over me. Meanwhile, I would love to hear from you. Since I'm not proficient in deciphering telepathic messages, please write to me via my Web site, www.sandrasteffen.com.

Until next time and always,

Sandra

For the newlyweds
Brad and Kelli

"For those who believe, no proof is necessary.
For those who don't believe, no proof is possible."
—Author unknown

Lila Delaney waited to look the detective in the eye until after he ushered her into the small, cluttered office at police headquarters in Hartford. He watched her closely as she took her seat at the marred, Formica-topped table. A second detective adjusted the blinds before dropping to the chair opposite her. They didn't believe what she'd told them over the phone.

"You said you know where Holly Baxter is," the first one said the instant introductions were out of the way.

Lila's reply was an anxious little cough that did nothing to alleviate the nerves jumping in her stomach. She hadn't expected this to be easy. After all, she wasn't a world-renowned psychic who could foretell the future. She simply had an unexplainable intuition that came in handy when helping her friends make career choices or find a lost pet. She'd never tried to help the police find a missing *person*. Of course, until this week, she'd never experienced a vision of this magnitude, and she'd certainly never ignored her own voice of reason, the one telling her to run, race, *bolt* in the opposite direction. Instead, here she was in Connecticut preparing to tell the authorities what she knew.

They wouldn't have agreed to her request for a meeting if their meager leads hadn't fizzled. The fact was, they were desperate to find Senator Charles Baxter's twenty-two-year-old daughter, Holly, who'd been missing for four days. Foul play was suspected, and everyone feared the worst.

"On the phone you said you saw Holly in your dreams." The older of the two, Lieutenant Owens was doing the talking, Detective Malone the smirking.

Lila couldn't decide who they reminded her of. Not Batman and Robin or the Lone Ranger and Tonto. Fred and Rickie? Ralph and Ed? Her longtime fiancé Alex Richardson often complained that she watched too much late-night television. He was due back from Dallas tomorrow. Surely if he were here, he would have tried to talk her out of this.

"Ms. Delaney?"

Hearing her name startled her. Recovering, she said, "My vision was similar to a dream, except I was awake when I saw her."

Owens strummed his fingers on the tabletop. Malone leaned back in his metal chair, bored. Lila could only sigh. Trying to make a nonbeliever believe was like trying to make a color-blind man see yellow, green and blue.

Leveling both men an I'm-not-enjoying-this-any-more-than-you-are stare, she said, "Look. I'm a busy psychologist with a successful practice. I didn't *have* to come here, and I want your word that you won't exploit me or my efforts to help." She waited for Owens to nod before she continued. "I believe Holly Baxter is being held in an old stone inn deep in the Hartford countryside."

The detectives couldn't help leaning ahead in their chairs. "What do you mean she's being held?"

"Her hands were cuffed."

"But she's alive?"

Lila had seen Holly Baxter writhing, an expression of intense pain on her young face. Closing her eyes on a feeling of deep and imminent sadness, she said, "I believe she is, yes."

"Where is this inn?" Malone asked, speaking for the first time.

This was the part Lila most dreaded trying to explain. "I don't know where it is, exactly."

"Oh, for crying out loud. She's wasting our time."

Malone was going to be no help whatsoever. Turning to his partner, Lila said, "I'm pretty sure I'll know it when I see it."

She wasn't the only one who was surprised when he said, "Let's go."

Twenty minutes later she was sitting in the passenger seat of an unmarked police car heading out of Hartford. Other than occasional static on the police radio, not a sound came from the interior of that car. Keeping her mind clear of doubt, she concentrated on the falling leaves and the shadows cast by the evening sun. Every so often she told Detective Malone to turn right or left. She lost the trail a few times, and had to ask him to turn around. Each time they neared an old house that had been converted into a bed-and-breakfast inn, he slowed slightly, waiting for her to say something.

At one point she happened to notice him looking in his rearview mirror. A bundle of nerves, she glanced over her shoulder in time to see a Channel 4 news van round the corner behind them. He swore under his breath, but it was too late to turn back because goose bumps skittered up and down her body, and her earlier vision shot through her mind.

"Turn here," she said louder than before.

He swerved. Barely keeping the car out of the ditch, he made a right onto Hampton Road.

"There," she said, motioning to a narrow driveway between crumbling stone pillars. Her stomach was on fire, and she felt an eerie sense of déjà vu as they pulled through the open gate.

"That looks like Holly's car," Detective Owens said, pointing to the back corner of a blue Beamer, all that was visible behind an overgrown hedge near the back of the property.

"Room number six," Lila whispered, squeezing her eyes shut against the image playing behind them.

"Stay here," Owens ordered, getting out. But she followed anyway.

Malone radioed for backup.

"And you—" Owens glared at the news team. "Stay out of the way or I'll throw you in jail for obstructing justice."

The news team gave the detectives a head start before closing in, leaves crunching with every step they took. Lila followed far more furtively.

"Police!" Malone yelled. "Open up."

A woman screamed.

Malone kicked in the door. He and Owens entered, pistols drawn. The cameraman crowded closer. Holly Baxter screamed again.

Peering around everyone else, Lila stared at the naked man in the king-size bed. "Alex?"

"Lila, what the hell?" He grabbed the sheet to cover himself.

"You're supposed to be in Dallas." Her voice seemed to come from far away.

"You know him?" Lieutenant Owens asked, his gun still pointed.

Holly Baxter nodded slowly.

And Lila heard herself say, "He's my fiancé." Shuddering violently, she added, "My ex-fiancé, it would seem."

Holly blushed scarlet. Alex looked shell-shocked. Somewhere, someone chuckled.

The room spun, and Lila spun with it. A strange silence was falling all around her. She felt herself falling, too, and all the while she was aware of the cameraman capturing everything on film.

CHAPTER 2

Six months later

The people gathered on the sidewalk in one of the oldest neighborhoods in Providence held morning newspapers and coffee mugs instead of microphones or cameras. They stood talking amongst themselves, two here, three there. There wasn't a member of the press among them. Lila Delaney was old news.

Two teenaged boys carried boxes containing all that remained of her life and her work here in Rhode Island. Everything fit neatly in the back of one compact U-Haul trailer.

A cheerless gray drizzle began to fall, sending the neighbors back inside their well-kept, closely spaced houses, so that only Lila and the young men wrestling her garden statues up the ramp of the rented trailer saw the taxi pull to a stop at the curb. One of the teenagers whistled under his breath as a svelte blonde dressed all in black got out. If anyone had been looking, they would have seen Lila's face brighten, too.

Penelope Bartholomew was always a sight for sore eyes.

Carrying herself with the regality inherent in the DNA of the naturally wealthy, Penelope, nicknamed Pepper years ago, stopped a few feet from Lila. "I go to Europe for eight months and all hell breaks loose for you."

Lila still cringed at the memory of her fast, humiliating and thorough downfall.

"They really sold T-shirts that said *My ex-fiancé, it would seem?*" Pepper asked after the two old friends had hugged.

Lila shuddered. "Coffee mugs, too." It had been the most coined phrase and biggest publicity circus since *Who Shot JR?* and *Where's The Beef?*.

"I can't believe you didn't call me."

"Would you have talked me out of it?" Lila asked.

"When have I ever been able to talk you out of anything?" Pepper's bright pink umbrella went up like a splash of color in a black-and-white photograph. Holding the umbrella over both of them, she said, "I recall talking you *into* a few things, though. Remember the time I persuaded you to attend that Harvard Fly Club party with me?"

Who could forget? Convinced her boyfriend was cheating on her, Pepper and Lila had gone dressed as guys. When they'd gotten caught, Pepper's parents had threatened to dissolve her trust fund over the incident. Although they would have liked to somehow blame it on Lila, they knew their daughter. Still, who could fault Mary Bartholomew for wanting her youngest to choose friends who came from old money and had grown up someplace suitable, such as the Cape or the Hamptons? Instead she'd brought home a waif from Chicago who had large hazel eyes and strange ideas about the universe.

Lila said, "We made quite an entrance that night, didn't we?"

Pepper nudged her with one shoulder. "If it hadn't been for your C cups, we would have fooled those fly-boys. But pooh grand entrances. I hear nobody makes grander exits than you, and on national television, no less."

Some grand exit.

Shuddering again, Lila turned her attention to the clanking and banging coming from the trailer. "Please be careful with Apollo. He belongs to my mother."

Pepper hid a yawn before saying, "There's a twenty in it for whichever one of you would be so kind as to move my bags from that taxi to the back-seat of Ms. Delaney's car."

While the quieter of the two fetched Pepper's bags, his friend said, "Are you here for a séance? Or are you pa-psychic, too?"

His cocky grin faded fast when Pepper stared at his fly and chanted something that sounded like a Romany curse. He loaded the last statue by himself, and barely waited for Lila's payment.

The moment the boys were gone, Lila said, "He has no idea you just told him you liked his shoes. For the rest of his life, he's going to believe any problem he has in bed is your fault."

"What man doesn't blame poor performance in the bedroom on a woman?"

Lila considered several clinical responses, then dismissed them all. Why bother? Her license was useless, her clinic as broken as she was. Taking a moment to note the dark circles beneath her friend's eyes, she said, "Mom sent you, didn't she?"

"You know your mother."

Yes, Lila knew her mother. Rose Delaney had come barreling into Providence in her '89 Buick as soon as the media frenzy exploded last fall. Despite the fact that she was five feet tall and wore house sweaters when it was ninety degrees outside, she'd parked herself in a rocking chair in Lila's living room, a big stick within easy reach, just in case a reporter tried to come through the door. She'd taken charge of the phone, too, and had shaken her fists at the curious passers-by, pointing her finger and shouting, "Shame on you."

Lila hadn't dared have the nervous breakdown she

deserved, if for no other reason than for fear of further upsetting her mother. But the night she'd overheard Rose telling someone from the Leno show, "Be kind to my girl, she's a sensitive, artistic soul," Lila had pulled herself together and told her mother she had to go home.

She *should* have known Rose would call Pepper. But Lila's intuition had self-destructed, or as one late-night comedian had put it, her mother-board had crashed.

"What are you really doing here, Pepper?"

"I'm going with you. Where are you going, anyway?"

"To Murray, Virginia, a little town in the Shenandoah Valley, but—"

"Murray, Virginia, prepare to meet two fierce, bad-ass, former Radcliffe girls!"

Lila tucked her shaking hands into her pockets and refrained from stating the obvious: these days, she was about as fierce as a day-old kitten.

She stepped into the drizzle and opened the car door. Pepper lowered the umbrella and slid into the passenger seat in seemingly one motion. The woman was liquid. At least one thing hadn't changed.

"You're serious?" Lila asked before starting her car. "You flew three thousand miles to make this trip with me?"

"Don't you want me to come with you? Far be it from me to go where I'm not wanted."

Since when? Lila thought, but she said, "I'll let you in on a little secret. Your arrival is the first thing that's happened these past six months that has anything to do with what I've wanted."

Shaking her head, Pepper said, "If your mother had her way, heads everywhere would roll. She'd start with the media, move on to the police, and then to some DA who doesn't believe in ESP. She has another fate in mind for your lying, cheating, no-good former fiancé. I never liked Alex."

Pepper didn't like most people, a trait that stemmed from being born rich and never knowing whom she could trust. Such were the problems of the filthy rich.

Casting one last look at the brownstone that had served as her home as well as the place she'd counseled patients these past ten years, Lila pulled away from the curb. It wasn't easy not to cry, but she'd already cried a river in that house.

"I believed I could help the police find that young woman," she said.

"The little hussy, you mean."

"I thought she was in trouble, and in pain. How was I supposed to know the reason she was writhing was because she was having sex with Alex?"

"It was probably more out of boredom than anything," Pepper said dryly.

"You can't imagine how much fun late-night comedians had at my expense."

"Want me to put rats in their closets and spiders in their pantries?"

Lila hadn't planned to smile. "You would do that for me?"

"What are friends for?" Lila and Pepper had spread their wings in opposite directions after college, but no matter how many miles or months separated them, something clicked each time they reunited. It was the kind of relationship they both accepted and appreciated. Moving her seat back to make room for her long legs, Lila's friend—perhaps the only friend she had left on the planet, said, "There are roughly five hundred miles between here and Murray, Virginia. That should give you plenty of time to tell me what happened. Start at the beginning. And, Lila, try not to leave anything out."

A horn blared. Lila jumped. And Pepper swore. In French. It was almost like old times.

"The speed limit on Skyline Drive is thirty-five, lady!" the balding driver of a huge motor home yelled as he passed.

Lila thought the horn was rude and the yelling was unnecessary. Gripping the steering wheel with both hands, she kept her eyes on the road and tried not to envision tumbling down the side of the mountain to a fiery death.

"We were just lapped by a camper van," Pepper said drolly. "How humiliating. You should let me drive. The last time was a fluke. Now that I've adjusted to being back in the States, I'm sure I'll remember to drive on the right side of the highway."

Lila was tired, but she wasn't *that* tired. Besides, there was no place to pull over. If she could have pried her hands off the steering wheel, she would have crossed herself. And she wasn't even Catholic. "I'm no stranger to humiliation, remember? I'm going to be fine eventually."

"Damn right you are."

"This is just a setback. I'm relatively intelligent."

"Relatively? You have a degree from one of the most prestigious universities in this country."

"In my experience," Lila said, "the two hundred million or so people living between New York and L.A. aren't terribly impressed by Ivy League degrees these days."

"What's this world coming to?"

Now there was a question.

"But, Lila, you and I both know you didn't do any of it for recognition."

Lila shrugged, for none of it mattered anymore. Her visions were gone, her peers weren't speaking to her, and no one wanted to be counseled by a woman who'd had no idea her fiancé was cheating. How could she have missed that?

She glanced in the rearview mirror. The eyes staring back at her were dull and somewhat blank.

The motor home took the next exit. Beyond it, the curves slackened and the highway began a gradual descent. The drive had been tedious and draining, but most of it was behind them, for they were over the mountains now, and were entering the Shenandoah Valley. Every inch of the descent brought a welcoming relief she hadn't expected.

The windows were down, and Lila was vaguely aware of a warm breeze and the lush rustle of leaves recently reborn. It reminded her that all was not lost. She had a destination and a place to live. The knowledge brushed at the emptiness. *She had a place to live*.

"Tell me more about this windfall of yours," Pepper said.

"There isn't much more to tell. It still seems incredible to me that Myrtle Ann Canfield left her property and all her worldly possessions to someone she never even met."

"Incredible? Maybe. Highly suspicious? Definitely."

Lila didn't like the sound of that, but she drove on, her little car diligently pulling her U-Haul trailer, down, down onto the rolling valley floor. There, two-lane roads meandered through quaint small towns named Fishers Hill, Lacey Spring, New Market and Weyers Cave. Between each town, roads curved and dipped past historic Civil War markers and poultry farms and apple orchards awash in white blossoms. It was all so utterly charming it almost made her believe it might be possible to find peace here.

She dug out the driving directions written in Myrtle Ann's own hand, and followed them to Old Cross Road. A sign at the corner read Murray, Virginia, 2 miles. Below it, *Welcome* had been stenciled, as if in afterthought. And beneath that someone had tacked a handwritten cardboard sign. *Parade Friday. 5:00. Don't be late.*

Lila stared at that welcome sign as if it had been written just for her. "I knew I could put my faith in Myrtle Ann."

"I still say there has to be a catch."

"I don't think a dead woman would lie." And then, because she wasn't sure of much anymore, Lila added, "Do you?"

"That's your area of expertise."

Some expert she'd turned out to be. "Myrtle Ann Canfield came into my life just as she was leaving her own, and in doing so she breathed hope where I needed it most. Because of her generosity, I'll live at The Meadows of Murray, the place Myrtle Ann cherished." She pictured it in her mind, a tranquil gentleman's farm with straight fences and rolling hills of pastures and a meandering stream. Perhaps she would raise horses, or maybe she would stretch a hammock between two trees and sleep the summer away. Sleep was definitely first on her agenda. Doctor's orders.

"That old woman didn't leave her property to just anybody," Pepper said. "She left it to you. She must have seen you on television, and probably read about you in the checkout lane. I'm your new voice of reason, and I'm telling you, a person doesn't leave her home and surrounding eighty acres to a perfect stranger out of the goodness of her heart. There has to be a string attached."

Lila didn't like the sound of that, either. Reminding herself that Pepper had always been a pessimist, she forced herself to focus on her driving as she followed Old Cross Road west. X marked the spot on Myrtle Ann's map. A faded shingle bearing letters barely discernible as The Meadows marked it at the side of the road.

The driveway was long and narrow, flanked on both sides by wind-battered oaks and willows. Perhaps in another lifetime it had been a working farm. Decades of storms had taken a toll on aging trees, and time on rotting fences. Mother Nature had been responsible for those changes. Lila wondered who was

responsible for the recent improvements, for some of
the fallen limbs had been cut, split and neatly stacked,
weeds mowed, new fence posts contrasting with old.

Chickens squawked, scattering out of the driveway
as Lila approached. A goat stood watch from the roof
of a rusting car. She counted two more junked cars
nearly covered by rambling roses, and other mounds
of debris hiding in weeds. Beyond the house were
several outbuildings weathered to a dull gray. In the
distance she saw more trees, a pond and what
appeared to be a small cabin.

Pulling to a stop near the main house, Lila got
out. She wondered if Pepper was right that Myrtle
Ann Canfield had left everything to her for a reason.
If so, what on earth could that reason be? Why not
leave her beloved homestead to someone stronger,
emotionally and physically? At the very least, why
not leave it to someone with enough money to finish
the clearing and mending?

Why her?

She tried to go to that place she used to go where
the air held a low vibration and the universe made
sense. Raising her gaze to the sky, she lowered it again,
her inner voice mute and her heart beating too fast.

Insects flitted and a soft evening breeze fluttered
weeds against her ankles. Spring had been stubborn
about arriving in the northeast. Here it already felt

like early summer. She stood in the fading twilight for a long time, staring at the house that was now hers. It was a sprawling two-story, its white paint peeling in places. Somebody had washed the windows and trimmed the rosebushes and planted flowers in front of the porch, as if in welcome. It was Lila's second welcome to Murray.

She tried the bottom step. When it held her weight, she took the next one. At the top, she made a sweeping survey of every inch of The Meadows in plain view. It was nothing as she'd envisioned, and yet it was a peaceful place, and peace was all she wanted or needed.

Key in hand, Lila unlocked the door. Without saying another word, she and Pepper went in.

Joe McCaffrey had seen the lights in the main house last night. He supposed it was inevitable that the peace and quiet wouldn't last, just as it was inevitable that the new owner would notice The Meadows had another resident.

He'd known Myrtle Ann had left the property to a woman from up north, a Yankee, she'd called her. That was all Myrtle Ann had had to say on the subject.

Seeing the new owner picking through boxes in her U-Haul trailer last night, he'd kept his lights off. This morning he faced the fact that he couldn't keep his presence a secret indefinitely. Before she got spooked and called the police—that was all Joe needed—he washed up and changed. He even shaved, although why he bothered, he didn't know. Evidently it was important to look his best while being evicted.

He'd been staying in this old cabin by the pond almost two years now. It had an antiquated refrigerator and stove, running hot and cold water, a huge monstrosity of a bed, one table, two chairs, one bathroom, one mirror, which was one mirror too many most days.

Staring at his reflection this morning, he rolled up his shirtsleeves, then held his right hand palmside up, slowly squeezing his fingers into a fist around an imaginary ball. The tendons in his wrist tensed and the muscles in his forearms coiled in anticipation.

He could almost hear the fans, thousands of them. "J.J.," they'd called him. His mother had called him Joe-Joe, short for Joseph John McCaffrey Jr. To everyone else who'd known him growing up in Murray, he'd always been Joe. Not just Joe. Joe-the-boy-wonder-McCaffrey, Murray High's all-star pitcher. He'd starred in college, too, and then during a short stint in the minors, followed by his lifelong dream, the majors. One thing had led to everything, and everything was what he'd had: a beautiful wife, beguiling daughter, thriving career, home, hearth and happiness. It was all gone now, except his daughter, but she'd changed, too. Who could blame her? Murray, Virginia, wasn't exactly a forgiving kind of town, and it sure as hell never forgot.

The signs marking yesterday's parade route had gone up all over town a week ago. Signs were unnecessary. The route hadn't changed in fifty years. But Murray was big on tradition, and it was a tradition to put up signs. The theme every year was the same, too. Peace in the valley. For a long time he'd been part of the tradition, riding in the parade with some of his old high school teammates when his schedule allowed.

He scowled, not because he'd lost his place in the limelight, but because he'd lost everything else. All because Noreen went missing one day. Husbands were always prime suspects in such cases. It didn't matter that there wasn't enough evidence for a trial. There wasn't even a body. A trial wasn't necessary in Murray, and living within spitting distance of the town's suspicions was both his punishment and their comeuppance.

To hell with it and to hell with them.

Staring hard at his reflection, at his narrowed eyes and the furrow between them, at the grim line of his mouth and the stubborn set of his chin, he flung the towel over the bar and tucked in his shirt. Peace. His scowl deepened as he headed up to the main house to introduce himself.

Joe Schmoe.

CHAPTER 3

Joe knocked on the front door, the side and the back. Cradling his sore knuckles, he backed up, oh for three.

He was trying to do the right thing. The car and trailer were parked in the driveway. Where was she?

When Myrtle Ann was alive, he'd always rapped twice before entering. She'd never locked her doors, and knocking had simply been a courtesy, for despite waning eyesight and an increasing dependence on her canes, the old woman always knew he was there. Said she could smell him the way she could smell an approaching storm.

Myrtle Ann Canfield had been a cagey old bird, an odd duck by Murray standards, a case of the pot calling the kettle black if there ever was one. Old age had shrunk her body and lined her face so deeply she'd looked a hundred for as long as Joe had known her. She'd never been one for gossip, preferring quiet companionship to idle chatter. Every once in a while she'd let something personal slip. Looking back, he realized those instances had been more carefully orchestrated than he'd realized at the time. She'd buried her husband fifty years ago and never seen fit to remarry. She and Joe had understood one another there. She hadn't had an easy life, but she'd once said it had suited her.

He hadn't expected to miss her.

But she was gone, and some law firm in Rhode Island had commissioned the local locksmith to change the locks in the main house when someone new inherited the old place. Joe had most likely already overstayed his welcome. No matter what they said about possession being nine-tenths of the law, the cabin by the pond wasn't his.

Hoofs clattered up the steps, and the world's most ornery goat butted Joe from behind. Giving the animal a guiding shove, he said, "Get off the porch, Nanny. Go on. You know better."

"So her name's Nanny."

The soft, plaintive sound drew Joe around. The woman stood in the doorway, her light brown hair hanging past her shoulders. He couldn't tell how old she was, mid- to late thirties, maybe. She was barefoot and sleepy-looking, her dress long and loose and the color of burnished copper. Over her shoulders she wore a sweater that was severely wrinkled, as if she'd just pulled it from a packing crate. Slipping her arms into the sleeves, she said, "She wouldn't tell me."

"Who?" he asked.

"The goat. You called her Nanny."

He found himself staring at the open door, puzzled. "That old relic is solid mahogany and has been sticking for years. How did you open it soundlessly?"

"Some things respond best to a gentle touch."

Something erotic seared the back of his mind. Dousing it at the source, he looked at her again.

She pulled the door shut as quietly as she'd opened it and joined him on the side porch. "What are the others' names?"

"The others?" he asked.

She motioned to the goats.

His father had been telling him he was becoming a hermit. Obviously, Joe had lost whatever paltry conversational skills he'd once had. He sure wasn't following her very well. But he tried. "That big one there? He's the only male. His name is Buck. The other two are Mo and Curly. Myrtle Ann's doings, not mine."

She seemed to take her time absorbing that. "Is there a Larry?"

He shook his head. They'd gotten off track. Drawing himself up and slightly away—how he'd gotten so close, he didn't know—he said, "I'm Joe McCaffrey. I've been looking after the place and feeding the animals for Myrtle Ann the past few years."

She nodded slowly without taking her eyes off him.

"Are you all right?" he asked.

He wouldn't have thought it was a difficult question, but she swallowed and took her sweet time replying. "Just really, really tired, so please don't feel obligated to kill me with kindness."

Kill her? Something inside Joe curled up like a sail furled inward. Did she know who he was? What people said? What it had cost him?

"It was a bad joke, Mr. McCaffrey."

The flatness was gone from her voice. In its place was a soreness he recognized all too well.

"I didn't mean to insult you by implying you're an ax murderer. I don't think Myrtle Ann would have let someone she didn't trust feed her animals."

A lot of people believed differently. Uneasy, he backed up a little more. Did she know or didn't she? She continued watching him, her hazel eyes guileless, causing him to wonder what, if anything, was going on behind them. "Are you sure you're all right?" he asked.

"Don't worry," she said, "I'm not a murderer, either."

The notion hadn't occurred to him. "That takes a load off my mind, ma'am."

The "ma'am" must have done it. Her eyes widened, and he saw a lighting in them. Maybe she *was* just tired. Not that it mattered. She wouldn't want him living in the cabin now that she owned the place.

"Do you have a name?" he asked.

"Everybody has a name, Mr. McCaffrey." She was looking at Myrtle Ann's goats as if she'd never seen farm animals up close.

Again, he waited. Finally, he decided to try another tack. "Have you had a chance to get acquainted with your own private piece of paradise?"

"I'm trying not to rush it."

She was teasing him. He had to look closely, but it showed in the softening of her mouth and the gentling of her expression.

A rooster crowed from the roof of a Studebaker nearly covered with vines. When the woman glanced at her watch, Joe felt compelled to explain. "That's Louie. His internal clock's a little off."

This time she smiled. "That sounds like my old college roommate. She's sleeping inside, still on Paris time. I take it you're also responsible for mending the fences and stacking that wood?"

He couldn't bring himself to ask her to consider letting him continue. To beg. A man had his pride. So instead, he went down the remaining steps and asked, "What are your plans?"

The question brought Lila up short. It occurred to her that she probably should have asked for some identification. Joe McCaffrey didn't *look* untrustworthy, and it was obvious that he was trying to keep a respectable distance between them. Extremely polite, he wore battered work boots and blue jeans faded nearly white at the major stress points: knees, seat and fly. His T-shirt was gray, his cropped hair the color of freshly ground coffee beans. There were three lines across his forehead and two more framing his upper lip. The lower half of his face was shiny, as if he'd shaved before coming over. He'd taken some trouble with his appearance before meeting her. That said something about him. She wasn't sure what.

How did people do this? How did they make assessments, judgments and decisions without the universe's input?

Lila had come to Virginia to learn.

"My plans?" she asked, wondering how long it had been since he'd asked the question.

"What are you going to do with the place now that it's yours?" he asked.

"I've been thinking a lot about that. Myrtle Ann Canfield was a generous woman."

"Yes, she was," Joe said quietly.

They stared at each other. He was the first to shift awkwardly, drawing away.

One of the goats butted a post. The chickens clucked nearby and the rooster crowed again in the distance. Lila felt overwhelmed. "I'm a city girl."

"Not anymore."

She pondered that. From here she could see much

of her property. There was a stand of pines to the west and a cabin near a pond, and a rowboat was tied to a dock. The grass had been mowed around the cabin just as it had been around the main house. Despite the recent improvements, orderliness began and ended there. She'd envisioned a gentleman's farm with painted white barns and fields of grain swaying in the breeze and perhaps a small garden where vegetables grew in neat rows and hills where fruit trees stood watch like guards of the property. Instead, The Meadows was overgrown and unkempt, animals roamed freely and a rooster crowed long past dawn. She wasn't quite sure what part Joe McCaffrey played in all of this. He seemed standoffish and emotionally wounded. But who wasn't?

"I have no idea how to care for these animals."

"It isn't difficult."

"Would you show me?" she asked.

A muscle worked in his cheek. "Before I clear out, you mean?"

"Clear out?"

He gestured to the cabin. "I've been living there almost two years now."

She stored the information. This inheritance may have been a godsend, but it hadn't come without responsibilities. The trip had exhausted her, and she had no idea what she was supposed to do next. She tried to go to that place she used to go where white energy radiated and the universe was orderly and systematic and she simply knew. When she'd lost her intuitive abilities and they'd declared her a fraud, the late-night television moguls had joked that there was a hole in her cosmos.

Maybe there was.

"I need help."

"Do you need a doctor?" Joe asked.

Feeling herself blushing, she wondered how long she'd zoned out this time. "Not that kind of help." Goodness, she was going to scare him away. Suddenly she was terrified she already had. "I was referring to the animals and all the rest."

He studied her, causing her to remember she hadn't combed her hair. She only hoped he could see past her bare feet and dishevelment.

"I would appreciate it if you would consider continuing whatever arrangement you had with Myrtle Ann." When he said nothing, she prodded, "Would you?"

"You aren't asking me to leave?"

"You don't want to leave?"

She held her breath.

He held her gaze.

For the first time she noticed that his eyes were brown. All three lines in his forehead were engaged in his scowl.

Shaking his head as if to clear it, he said, "I'll stay." And then, more quietly, "For now."

Relief rained down on her. Before she started laughing uncontrollably, she turned toward the door, but changed her mind. Instead of going inside, she eased around the corner of the house and back onto the side porch where she could watch him walk away.

"Mr. McCaffrey?" she called after some time had passed.

Turning, he faced her, feet apart, hands on his hips.

"Since I can't restore order to the universe, I'm going to restore it to The Meadows. This was once a working farm. I think it needs to be again. Do you think Myrtle Ann would mind?"

"She left it to you, didn't she?"

"I hope that hasn't caused problems for you."

"Believe me, it was no skin off my nose."

She stared at him, and Joe found it unnerving. The breeze fluttered the hem of her skirt and lifted her hair away from her face. She looked like someone from one of the old legends that abounded in the valley. He was pretty sure she was smiling.

"I'm very glad to be here," she said, "And I'm pleased to make your acquaintance."

She slipped soundlessly out of sight around the corner of the house before he thought to mention that he still didn't know her name. By then it was too late. He should have told her about the rumors. It was too late for that, too. Besides, it was only a matter of time before she went into town and heard them for herself. Wondering if she would still want him living in her cabin then, he continued on toward the pond. For the hell of it, he picked up a stone and flung it, sending it skipping across the surface on his way by. He heard it skip across the water, but he didn't stick around to count the ripples or watch the stone sink.

The old-fashioned screen door bounced as it closed behind him. Looking around, he caught his reflection in the mirror inside. After a time, he shrugged, for it was official. The new owner of The Meadows of Murray was a loon.

She was going to fit right in.

"So you're the new owner of The Meadows."

It was the third time it had been said in exactly that way, the third time Lila and Pepper exchanged a quick look, the third time Lila nodded.

The cashier at the grocery store had watched them closely as she'd said, "I heard somebody new was moving in."

The attendant at the gas station where she'd dropped off the U-Haul trailer and filled up her gas tank had asked what she planned to do with the place. Like the others, the waitress leaning in to take their orders right now said, "Have you met Joe yet?"

Pepper's sharp kick under the table kept Lila from replying.

"Lila and I don't quite know what to make of him."

"Then you've heard."

Pepper smiled encouragingly at the waitress. Again, Lila felt a sharp nudge under the table.

Joe McCaffrey had unloaded the trailer while Pepper slept. After a brief discussion, he and Lila had decided that he would stack everything except the garden statues on the back porch until she made room in the house. He hadn't come inside, and Pepper hadn't ventured out.

"Nobody wanted to believe it at first," the waitress exclaimed. "Not of one of our own."

Pepper shook her head. "I can only imagine how you must have felt."

While Lila pulled a face, one of the other customers called, "Trudy, can I get a refill up here?"

The heavyset waitress tucked her pencil over her ear and said, "I'll be right back."

Rubbing her sore shin, Lila waited until Trudy was out of hearing range to whisper, "You haven't met Joe."

"Trudy doesn't know that." Pepper had slept hard. Despite the crease still lining one cheek and the traces of jet lag in her voice, she was suddenly wide awake. "She's dying to tell us something. Who are we to deny her?"

Lila felt a vague sense of unease. She didn't like gossip, but Pepper was right about one thing. Everyone they'd encountered seemed to want to tell them something about Joe.

She and Pepper had found this little diner on Rebellion Street in the middle block of the downtown district of Murray. The courthouse claimed the most prominent position at the head of the town square, the post office and usual law and insurance offices nearby. Evidently, the chains hadn't made it this deep into the Valley, for there wasn't a Starbucks or Baby Gap to be found. Instead, there was a charming old-fashioned five-and-dime, a card and gift shop, a bookstore, three bars, a dress boutique and a huge antique store. Lila would have enjoyed browsing, but Pepper had needed coffee, industrial strength, which reminded Lila. "You haven't touched your latte."

Pepper took a cursory sip. "Here she comes. Let me handle this."

The waitress returned, topping off their water glasses and spreading the cutlery. "Where was I?"

"You were telling us how nobody could believe it about Joe." Pepper's tone invited trust.

Falling for it, Trudy said, "It may have been a crime of passion, but murder is murder, isn't it?"

Not even Pepper could form a coherent reply.

Trudy didn't seem to need one. "We all assumed he would leave town after, well, you know, after the body never turned up. Instead, Myrtle Ann asked him to come live at The Meadows. The place went to seed for more than twenty years. Stone walls crumbled and more limbs fell with every passing storm. Out of the blue, she asked Joe to start clearing the pastures. Some people think she knew she was dying. Went to her maker on her way back from the mailbox. Folks still find pieces of her mail spread far and wide by the wind that day. It was junk mail mostly, beggin' letters, she used to call them. She must have sent a donation to every charitable organization on the planet. A lot of people wondered if she'd have any money left." Trudy looked at Lila shrewdly. "Are you a relative of Myrtle Ann's?"

Lila floundered. How could she tell this woman that she'd never even met Myrtle Ann Canfield? It was Pepper who finally answered. "Lila has an interesting family tree, but at least her family doesn't treat her like a puppet on a string the way mine does. Getting back to Joe, why do you suppose Myrtle Ann asked him to start clearing the pastures?"

"You know how old people get," Trudy said. "Joe took good care of her, I'll give him that."

"Joe McCaffrey, a suspected murderer." Pepper

made a *tsk, tsk* sound. "I've read that a lot of serial killers are good to their mothers. Ow. I mean, ooh la la." It was Pepper's turn to rub her sore shin.

Trudy peered in both directions before lowering her voice, but even her whisper was strong enough to penetrate steel. "They say he hasn't set foot in his house since it happened."

"Why do you suppose that is?" Pepper asked.

"Guilt, most likely. The police finally took down the yellow tape they'd strung around his big, fancy house just west of town. Poor Chloe. Her mother missing and her father the prime suspect in the case." Trudy shook her head. "She must be thirteen now. Hardly ever comes home from that fancy boarding school Noreen sent her to before she *disappeared*. Can't say I ever liked the woman myself. That doesn't make it right, does it? It's always the husband, though, isn't it? It's a shame, such a shame. He was our star, too. Had an arm on him like nobody else. Man, that boy could pitch. Went pro practically right out of college. He always did have a temper. Guess it got the best of him."

Someone called Trudy's name, and the waitress was forced to get back to work. Stirring more cream into her coffee, Pepper all but gloated. Lila didn't like what her friend was thinking, and it had nothing to do with psychic awareness.

"I believe we've just stumbled upon Pearl Ann's string."

Although it went against her better judgment, Lila said, "Her name was Myrtle Ann, not Pearl Ann."

Pepper patted her mouth with her napkin. "A burned-out baseball player with a missing wife and an intuitionist who needed a place to go. Quite a coincidence, wouldn't you say?"

"I'm not an intuitionist anymore. What good could I be to a man suspected of killing his wife?" Lila felt a heavy, sinking feeling, as if she were being sucked into something she couldn't control or foresee.

"Gretel Ann was brilliant."

"*Myrtle Ann* was brilliant, you mean."

Pepper smiled, victorious. Picking up her coffee again, Pepper had the good sense to wipe the grin off her face.

It saved Lila the trouble.

CHAPTER 4

"Pepper, what are you doing?"

"I'm checking to see if Joe's cabin's locked. What does it look like I'm doing?"

Lila glanced nervously over her shoulder because that was exactly what it looked like Pepper was doing. "Did you hear something?" She wished she hadn't kept her voice so quiet. It made her feel like a conspirator.

"Relax," Pepper said. "Joe isn't home, remember?"

Relax? On each of the five days since their arrival, Lila had taken relaxing walks through the orchard, along the lane and into the back pasture. She wasn't sure why she'd refrained from making the pond and cabin a destination, but she most certainly was not relaxed about what Pepper was proposing. "We can't go inside."

"Sure we can."

"It's trespassing," Lila insisted. "For your information, I have every intention of leaving the note on the door."

"For your information, one can't trespass on one's own property. You might as well put the note inside, out of the weather."

Lila squinted into the sun. "Out of what weather? It's another glorious day."

But Pepper wasn't listening. "It isn't locked. Aren't you curious about how a man who killed his wife lives?"

"We don't know he killed his wife."

"We don't know he didn't. No one's heard from Noreen McCaffrey in two years. Not even her own daughter. Not so much as a peep."

"They haven't found Noreen's body," Lila said. "Maybe she's alive."

"Then where is she?"

That was the million-dollar question.

Pepper went inside, her loose-fitting black summer slacks and tank fading into the shadows. Drawing the door closed, Lila taped the note to it and called through the screen in a nearby window, "What if he catches you?"

"He's established his pattern." Pepper's voice grew muffled. "Every day he works on fences or buzzes through tree limbs or hauls away junk from nine in the morning until four-thirty in the afternoon. And then he goes somewhere, and we don't see his lights come on until the wee hours of the morning."

Lila had to take Pepper's word for that, because she'd been sound asleep at that time of the night. She used to be a night owl, but since her public disgrace on national television, she'd taken to going to bed early.

"There isn't much in here," Pepper called. "Just some old furniture and a stove right out of the dark ages."

Lila knew better than to ask her what she'd expected. After listening to the local gossip on Saturday, they'd visited an old schoolhouse-turned-library where they'd discovered a vast though unorganized collection of newspaper and magazine articles regarding Noreen McCaffrey's disappearance and the investigation that had followed. There were several quotes from highly respected people and some damning evidence pointing directly at Joe. Like most people, Pepper had a morbid fascination with it all. Staring at those grainy photographs had left Lila with the lingering feeling that she was looking at a part of someone's life that should have remained private.

Although she'd seen Joe from a distance several times, they hadn't come face-to-face since that initial meeting the morning after her arrival. Lila had spent her time since then either sleeping or getting acquainted with the animals and the farm. By Wednesday, she'd grown bored with long walks and decadent naps, and had aired the house and begun the arduous task of sorting through drawers and boxes of Myrtle Ann's old letters, receipts and recipes. Much of it was tedious, but it kept her busy. Until her brief and humiliating jaunt into police identification work, she'd operated a counseling clinic where people came and went all day long. She'd never been rich, and her savings account was dwindling. She missed helping her patients discover ways to fix the problems in their lives. It was too bad she had no idea how to fix the problems in hers.

"Is something wrong?"

She could have handled the deep voice spoken so close to her ear, but the large hand on her shoulder sent Lila straight into the air. Heart pounding, she spun around and tried to breathe.

Joe McCaffrey stood between her and the sun, a muscle working in one cheek. Other than a small splash in the pond behind him, the early evening was quiet.

Lila could only imagine how this must look. "I didn't hear you drive up."

"I parked by the big house. I tried knocking. Now I know why you didn't answer."

"I was just leaving you a note."

He reached for the sheet of stationery taped to his door, his forearm brushing her hair. He went perfectly still at the contact, his face two feet from hers, his gaze going from her eyes, to her mouth, and finally away.

He drew back far enough to open the note and scan it. Stuffing it into his back pocket, he said, "You might as well come in."

He eased around her and gave the door a little

push. If he noticed it hadn't been latched, he didn't mention it as he went in.

It was only after she followed him inside that she spared a thought for Pepper. From her position near the door, she could see most of the interior. The kitchen and living areas were separated by a wood-stove open to both rooms. Three doors led from the main area. One was closed, and the other two rooms appeared to be a rustic bathroom and a bedroom. There was no sign of Pepper anywhere.

Lila heard the clank of an old-fashioned refrigerator opening and closing. Moments later Joe returned with a two-quart jar in his hand.

"Bud Streeter drank his last paycheck again. His oldest boy sweeps floors and washes glasses at McCaffrey's Tavern. He won't let me give him money he hasn't earned, but he takes the goats' milk home to his two younger brothers. I planned to run it by you first, now that the place is yours."

She had trouble talking around the lump that had formed in her throat. "That's fine. Of course it's fine."

Neither of them seemed to know what else to say.

He finally gestured for her to precede him. Outside, he said, "Don't worry about your friend. She sneaked out the back door while you were guarding the front."

Lila stopped in her tracks. Joe didn't stop at all.

Hurrying to catch up, she considered apologizing.

Discarding several explanations, she finally opted for the simple facts. "Pepper and I will be gone for a few days." She had to practically run to keep up. Wanting to explain, she said, "She's convinced we both need a project. She's researching a career change."

If he spoke, it was lost in the breeze. After that, she conserved her energy for the fast trek. They went their separate ways where the driveway forked, she up her porch steps, he to his Jeep parked in the shade.

"Mr. McCaffrey?" she asked as he opened the Jeep's door. "May I call you Joe?"

He turned to look at her, one foot on the ground, the other on the running board. Taking his pause as a yes, she said, "I think it's nice, what you're doing for that boy and his family."

He seemed as surprised as he was uncomfortable with the praise. Just when she'd given up all expectation of receiving any kind of reply, he said, "I hope your friend's career change doesn't involve spy work or private investigation."

For some reason, she smiled. "So do I."

He glanced back the way they'd come before saying, "I would have locked the door if I'd wanted to keep people out."

Obviously a man of few words, he got in and drove away.

Watching the trail of dust on the road, Lila

thought about that goat's milk and Joe's unlocked doors. In the back of her mind, she wondered if she dared believe that actions spoke louder than words.

Joe wiped the pretzel crumbs and cigarette ashes off the counter, cringing slightly when he reached too far. The soreness in his arms and shoulders was almost welcome, for it gave him a focus other than the announcer's voice booming over the TV.

The usual Thursday night crowd was here, a dozen in all. That number would double on Friday and Saturday, and by Sunday it would taper off to five or six. McCaffrey's Tavern had been in Joe's family for four generations, as much a tradition in Murray as the ball game droning from a high shelf behind the counter.

He'd grown up on the second bar stool from the left, his feet swinging as he slurped root beers and crunched on bar nuts, his eyes trained on the baseball players who'd seemed larger than life. He had precious few memories of his mother, who'd died when he was six. His father had raised him, and people used to say he'd done a damn good job of it. Opinions had a way of shifting overnight. Joe Sr. still helped out at the bar most afternoons, but these days his step was heavier and his shoulders stooped.

"Swing and a miss!" The announcer drew the call out the way announcers always did.

It never used to annoy Joe.

It was the bottom of the fourth. The Cougars were behind, and everyone in the tavern was grumbling about it.

A hush fell suddenly. Joe looked up, straight at the reason. Lila Delaney and her friend were sauntering toward him.

The next batter took a practice swing; the poker game continued at the back table, but Joe wasn't fooled. Every person in the room kept one eye trained on the two women sidling up to the bar.

The blonde wore red, Lila beige chinos and a soft-looking knit shirt the color of walnut shells. Keeping her voice too low for anyone else to hear, she said, "Pepper has something she wants to say to you."

Pepper Bartholomew leaned closer. "Lila wasn't guarding the door. Not that it wouldn't have been nice."

Lila nudged her.

And Pepper said, "I owe you an apology. I'm sorry you caught me snooping."

She winked, causing Joe to wonder if she was apologizing for snooping or for getting caught. If she hadn't been so upper-crust, he would have called her expression sassy. She was taller than Lila and probably paid a small fortune for the clothes, the manicure, the platinum jewelry and that perfectly tousled hairstyle.

"Hey, sweetheart," Bud Streeter said, doing something disgusting with his tongue. "Why don't you bring a little of that honey down my way?"

Joe wouldn't have wanted to be on the receiving end of Pepper's arctic glare. Not that Bud didn't deserve worse.

"Would either of you ladies care for a drink?" Joe asked, quietly diverting their attention. "On the house."

"Perhaps another time," Pepper said before steering Lila back the way they'd come.

At the door, Lila looked over her shoulder at Joe. The smile she gave him felt like a small act of kindness in a vicious world.

As talk resumed throughout the bar, Bud slid his empty glass across the counter. "Looks like you've got yourself a couple'a new pieces of ass to choose from."

"Watch it, Bud," one of the women patrons warned through a haze of cigarette smoke.

Bud's laugh was derogatory and grating. "The blonde's flashier. Probably be fun to ride. But the brunette's got a bigger rack. That one looks familiar." He bit into a pretzel. "Don't that one look familiar? Where have I seen her?"

Drunk or sober, Bud Streeter was a mean man. Joe would have liked to ban him from the bar, but at least when Bud was here, he wasn't getting trashed in front of the television in his trailer and yelling obscenities at his three boys. If it hadn't been for those three innocent kids, Joe wouldn't have blamed Bud's wife for leaving him.

Picturing his own little girl in his mind, Joe felt a pang of remorse and regret. Chloe was thirteen, and he hardly knew her anymore. A bar was no place to raise a daughter. She was better off with her friends, her teachers and the headmistress at her boarding school in Philadelphia. She would probably grow up sophisticated and smart, and none of the credit would be his.

Joe looked around McCaffrey's. The room was long and narrow, with low ceilings, dark-paneled walls and darker corners. The clientele paid cash and didn't tip. They hadn't been impressed when he'd made the majors, and they didn't care what people said about him now any more than they cared about anything else. It wasn't that they were down on their luck. Most had jobs; some had families. What they lacked was life.

This damn sure wasn't the life he'd chosen.

Once, he'd had dreams. These days, his contribution to society was putting up with snide comments from the biggest loser in town.

The notion made him pause. When had he stopped thinking of *himself* as the biggest loser in town?

Something warm and wet grazed Joe's neck.

Fighting his way through layers of sleep, he rolled over, the sheet tangling around his legs. As he did every night after work, he'd driven back to the cabin and stood in the shower, letting the warm water carry the secondhand cigarette smoke and grime down the drain. Leaving the low window open by his bed, he'd crawled naked between the sheets, seeking oblivion.

Again, warm lips nuzzled his neck.

Easing away from those soft kisses, he groaned. Although daylight was trying to penetrate his eyelids, he wasn't ready to wake up. He turned away from another wet kiss, then slipped back to sleep, wondering who'd sneaked into his hotel room this time. It must have been one hell of a game, because his whole body hurt. He always ached after a game, his pitching arm and shoulder especially. The party afterward must have been intense, because he couldn't even remember who they'd played.

Whoever was in his bed with him was persistent.

"Sorry, honey," he mumbled. "I'm married."

Damn groupies, anyway.

Reality landed hard in his mind. Bolting upright, he clambered out of bed so fast the tangled sheet came with him. One of Myrtle Ann's goats watched from the open window.

"Damn it, Curly!"

The stupid goat licked the windowsill, and Joe cursed again. Erasing from his mind all memory of the erotic dream from hell, he reached for his boots and jeans.

* * *

Lila was closing the gate when she noticed Joe leading the last missing goat by a leash fashioned from his belt. "Thank goodness you found her," she said. "I managed to get these three back in the corral and was wondering where that one had gone."

He put the goat with those already inside the enclosure. The others frolicked, but the white one nuzzled Joe, who moved away, out of its reach.

"I think she has a crush on you."

He mumbled something unintelligible under his breath then clamped his mouth shut. An awkward silence followed.

Finally, she said, "Pepper and I got back late last night. Neither of her business ventures turned out as she'd hoped."

"She had two?"

"There's an arena football team for sale in South Carolina and an alpaca ranch for sale right here in Virginia."

"Does she know anything about football or alpacas?"

"Well, no, but that never stopped her in the past. Clinically, she's the spoiled daughter of extremely wealthy parents. She has two perfect older sisters, a workaholic father, a perfectionist mother and a controlling grandfather."

"Just your average all-American family."

Lila was tempted to smile. The sun had burned off the fog here, but it swirled in the foothills in the distance, filtering light and obscuring the mountains from view.

Resting his forearms on the fence he'd recently mended, Joe said, "A few nights ago, Bud Streeter recognized you. I didn't tell him he was right, but I thought you should know. Word's out."

"It isn't exactly a secret. The media made sure of that. How long have you known?"

"It took me a few days to place where I'd seen you. I catch a lot of late-night TV at the tavern."

"It seems we're both famous," she said.

"More like infamous."

They looked at each other, both curious, but neither willing to voice their questions out loud.

Eventually, Joe said, "Not much happens in small towns, but what you hear makes up for it."

"This is my first exposure to life in a small town. Myrtle Ann must have seen me on television. Pepper thinks that's why she left The Meadows to me. You cared for her and this property. I don't understand why she didn't leave it to you."

"I don't need it. Noreen's disappearance cost me my reputation, my concentration and my future, but I'm far from destitute."

Turning her back on the animals, Lila surveyed her

new home. The rising sun backlit the uneven lines of the house and accentuated the sag in the porch roof. The imperfections made the house look almost human, like lines on a wizened old woman's face. Standing near the fence, the breeze in her hair and dew wicking into her canvas shoes, she'd never been so appreciative of someone she'd never met. "Thanks to Myrtle Ann, I'm not destitute, either."

"Still," he said, "now that people know who you are, they're going to talk. The former psychic and the burned-out baseball player suspected of killing his wife."

After another awkward silence, Lila said, "As long as it's just idle gossip."

Why that struck either of them as funny, she didn't know, but she started to laugh, and so did he. Once they started, neither could stop. She snorted embarrassingly. He roared, even more out of practice than she was. They were bad at laughing. It made them laugh harder, until they were holding their stomachs, chests heaving, guffawing until they hurt. Oh, it felt good.

Lila had often counseled patients through grief and despair. How many times had she reassured them that one day they would be able to laugh again and mean it?

"My mother is going to be happy to hear I've taken my own advice," she said, drying her cheeks with her fingertips.

She wound up telling Joe about the times her

mother had stood up to obnoxious reporters and Lila's former patients who'd threatened to sue. Looking back, she didn't know how she would have gotten though the ridicule and media circus without her fierce, slight, eccentric mother.

Lila had read the newspaper accounts of Joe's baseball career and his volatile relationship with his wife. She knew he had a daughter, but she didn't recall reading anything about any extended family. As a counselor, and as an only child, she was always curious about families. "Do you have any brothers or sisters?"

"Just my dad and my daughter. Neither of them are one hundred percent certain I didn't do it."

She could have done quite well without that particular bit of information. She must have looked at him for a long time, because he glanced nervously at her, prompting her to ask the question on her mind. "Why did you move here?"

"What do you mean, why?"

"You have a beautiful house in Murray. From what I hear, it has every imaginable luxury."

He stared across the meadows, past the fruit trees and the pond, to the mountains, more visible now. "Noreen had to have that house, so I had it built for her. There's nothing for me there. Besides, it doesn't have this."

Lila was looking at him, not the view. "There's no peace there," she said quietly.

A muscle worked in his jaw. "That's right, there isn't."

She understood, and it should have scared her. The fact that it didn't should have sent her sprinting back to the house. Instead, she watched him walk away.

It didn't take him long to reach the pond. He picked up a stone on his way by, and with a flick of his wrist that was probably second nature, he sent it skipping across the water. Strangely, he didn't stick around to count the skips or watch it sink.

The screen door bounced three times, but Lila didn't take her eyes off the pond. The water glinted in the morning sunshine, the surface now rippling in five places, spreading outward in a perfect, silent rhythm, propelled by a force too gentle to feel and too powerful to control. By the time the ripples touched the grassy edges on all sides, the middle was smooth again. Like those ripples, Joe was a power unto himself, too. Maybe everyone was.

She came out of her stupor to see that Pepper was on the porch. Tall, svelte and sleepy-looking, her friend stared toward the cabin, a quilt wrapped around her shoulders, both hands around a cup of steaming coffee. "There went one fine specimen of a man. It almost wouldn't matter if he did it."

"I don't think he did."

Pepper turned her head slowly, her short blond hair sticking up on one side. "Oh no?"

Not one to waste precious energy on pretense, Lila only shrugged.

"You're falling for him," Pepper said.

"I wouldn't go that far."

"Think about it, Lila. He has nothing to offer you, at least nothing except heartache, and maybe an early death."

"It's not as if I'm planning to propose. Believe me, Alex cured me of the very idea of marriage. I just don't think Joe hurt his wife."

"Why don't you ask him?" Pepper said. "No, wait, the police already did."

"And he said he didn't kill Noreen."

"I'd say that, too," Pepper grumbled.

"I think he's telling the truth."

"Oh, God."

Lila shrugged all over again.

"He's dangerous, Lila."

She didn't think so. What's more, for the first time in months, she felt revived and regenerated, not in a psychic sense, but in a living, breathing, female sense. "If you believe he killed Noreen, why are you still here?" she asked, joining Pepper on the porch. "Why aren't you afraid?"

Pepper didn't seem to know what to say.

"That's what I thought," Lila said. "Besides, you're the one who told me I needed a project."

Letting the quilt slip from her shoulders, Pepper said, "So take up knitting or go back to school. If anything happens to you, your mother is going to have me drawn and quartered."

"Nothing's going to happen to me." Scooping up the quilt and handing it back to Pepper, Lila added, "You're staying, then?"

Pepper followed her inside, muttering all the way to the kitchen where she topped off her coffee. "I've been meaning to talk to you about that. It seems I'm, or rather, I'm not, um, let's just say I've run into a little difficulty regarding my finances."

"What sort of difficulty?"

Pepper pulled a face. "My family has cut me off."

"You mean financially? What did they do? Freeze access to your trust fund? And you didn't tell me?"

Sighing, Pepper said, "You have enough problems of your own. Besides, it's only until I agree to assume my rightful place in the bowels of monotony. I told my grandfather not to hold his breath, and he told me to stop acting like a spoiled little heiress. At that point, I probably shouldn't have reminded him that I've been taller than him since I was thirteen."

Oh dear. Pepper's grandfather had a very serious

Napoleon complex. "He really froze access to your trust fund unless you do as he says?"

"And my dad's backing him up. My mother doesn't like it, but everyone knows Grandfather and Daddy run that show."

"You're welcome to stay as long as you need to, but I have to remind you I don't have much money, either."

"I know. I have a little money left in my emergency fund, but it's going fast. This may sound drastic," Pepper said, "But I think I'm going to have to get a job."

"You're going to go to work?"

"It isn't as if I don't want to work," Pepper said, justifiably defensive. "It's just that Kelly Rippa already has my dream job."

Lila made a clicking sound with her tongue. "There is no justice. But don't worry, we'll think of something." Suddenly this felt like old times, and she added, "We're in for an interesting summer, there's no doubt about that."

"If we're lucky," Pepper said drolly, "we might even both live to tell about it."

"I don't believe in luck."

"I know. You believe in destiny." Pepper sipped her coffee thoughtfully. "If we're destined to spend our summer here, we're going to need more information about Noreen McCaffrey."

We? Lila nudged her friend away from the coffee-pot and helped herself to a cup.

Pepper's expression was composed as she focused her attention on the situation. And Lila knew that even this early in the morning, Pepper was formulating a plan.

CHAPTER 5

When Lila was growing up, her mother often said she was too curious for her own good. Evidently, that hadn't changed. Why else would she stop what she was doing to answer the door?

The woman on her front porch wore a wide-brimmed hat and a tentative smile. "I'm Katherine Avery. You might have noticed my antique store on Rebellion Street. I understand you're interested in selling some of Myrtle Ann's pieces."

If the fiasco last fall had taught Lila anything, it was to proceed with caution. "What makes you think that?"

Katherine Avery removed her hat and fanned herself with it, the man-made breeze stirring her chin-length dark hair. "Your friend mentioned it to Trudy at the diner. Trudy told Ginny Calhoun. I believe it was Ginny who told Irene Motz, who was trying on the new nautical sweaters at the dress boutique while your friend was talking to Priscilla, the owner, about possibly working there. Regardless, it was Irene who first mentioned it to me."

Lila's dismay must have shown, because Katherine tilted her head slightly and said, "My mama used to say the rumor mill is the wireless telegraph in its purest form. May I come in?"

Feeling a surge of anticipation of something pleasant, Lila opened the door. Katherine came in as if she knew her way around. She examined a lamp on the hall table, a stack of old books, and finally the table itself, her hands gliding lovingly over surfaces, a finger touching here and smoothing there. When she came to a ledger Lila had discovered an hour ago, she leafed through pages of columns of amounts and prices of vegetables and fruit sold by the peck and bushel. "After Harlan died, Myrtle Ann supported herself from the proceeds of a fruit and vegetable stand. This is quite a find, you know."

It was only one of many such items Lila had come across. All morning she'd been going through bureau drawers and cubbies crammed to bursting with buttons, recipes, receipts, used wrapping paper and the mail. Once considered a personality quirk, psychologists today viewed hoarding as a symptom of a mental condition associated with obsessive-compulsive disorder. Lila was of the opinion that people who hoarded saw potential in everything.

Where would she be if Myrtle Ann hadn't seen the potential in her?

Sorting through all the clutter and chaos was bringing a sense of order and a deeper understanding of the former owner of The Meadows. It was an unusual way to get to know someone.

Katherine was looking at the tall armoire in the corner the way a mountain climber might look at Annapurna. Reverently placing her hand on the front panel, she said, "This has the original finish. Myrtle Ann always did know how to care for old treasures."

"Were you a friend of Myrtle Ann's?" Lila asked.

"In a way, perhaps, but she wasn't what you'd call a people person. Folks said she was crazy, you know."

"Was she?"

"Not any crazier than the rest of us." Katherine's gaze caught on her own reflection in an antique mirror and she seemed a bit startled.

"Is something wrong?" Lila asked.

"Sometimes I don't recognize myself." She colored slightly, as if she hadn't meant to say that out loud.

Experience and training kept Lila silent, but she continued to watch Katherine closely.

"I walk past a mirror, and I wonder, who is this person? I look vaguely familiar, but I bear little resemblance to the face I'm expecting. I miss—"

When it became apparent that she didn't plan to finish the statement, Lila asked softly, "What do you miss?"

Katherine seemed to be running through a mental checklist. "I suppose I miss the woman I thought I'd be by now."

"You miss the woman you thought you'd be and I miss the woman I thought I was. My situation forced me to remove my rose-colored glasses, but psychologists call the phenomenon you described as displacement of self. If I was still practicing, and you were my patient, I would tell you she's in there waiting for you to recognize her and reconnect."

"You're good," Katherine said.

"I used to charge a hundred dollars an hour for sharing my insight, and I just offered it to you free of charge. Did you really come out here because of Trudy or Priscilla or Ginny or what was her name? Irene?"

If she hadn't been looking, Lila would have missed the way Katherine schooled her expression before answering, "I have at least three customers who would pay dearly for that Dutch armoire alone. As long as I'm here, I might as well tell you I think Myrtle Ann was very wise to leave her home to you."

Lila didn't know what to say. She certainly hadn't expected that. "You said she kept to herself?"

"What little family Myrtle Ann had died a long time ago. I think Joe knew her better than anyone. A lot of folks wondered if you would turn him out when you arrived. I'm glad you didn't."

"You care what happens to Joe?" Lila had been so intrigued by the conversation she hadn't realized Katherine was leaving until she found herself on one side of the screen door, Katherine Avery on the other.

"Joe and my husband played baseball together in high school. He was the best man at our wedding."

That didn't really answer the question, but Katherine was gliding down the porch steps, calling "thank you" over her shoulder. "I hope you'll keep me in mind if you decide to part with that armoire or any of the other treasures. Stop by the store anytime. Have a good day."

Back in the living room, Lila wondered what that had been about. She didn't doubt Katherine's sincerity when it came to antiques. But she'd seemed to be guarding something. Or someone. Lila was still thinking about that when Pepper returned a few minutes later.

Dropping her Gucci bag on a table already stacked high with old newspapers, Pepper said, "That man doesn't like me."

"What man?" Lila looked up from the same piece of junk mail she'd been staring at for the last five minutes.

"Joe."

"You never think anybody likes you."

"Trust fund babies never know who they can trust. Ironic isn't it?"

Pepper's sigh contained all the drama of an Audrey Hepburn movie. It took Lila back to the day she and Pepper met during their freshman year at Radcliffe. Back then, Lila had spent most of her time studying so she wouldn't lose her scholarship, while Pepper spent her free time with other girls who had buildings and library additions named after their relatives. Needing a break from her studies, Lila had gone to the video store to rent a movie. She and Pepper both reached for the only copy of the 1948 version of *Anna Karenina*. It had been Pepper's idea to watch it together. Thanks to Vivien Leigh, they'd clicked. Discovering someone who didn't like her for her family's money was a novel experience for Pepper, but the friendship worked both ways.

"I didn't expect you back so soon," Lila said.

"Whoever said small-town people are big gossips hasn't visited Murray, Virginia, on a Monday morning in late May."

"No one wanted to talk to you?" Lila asked, incredulous.

"Difficult to believe, isn't it? Although now that you mention it, they were more than willing to share anecdotes and stories about moonshine and legendary fog so thick farmers have been known to turn it over with their plows without realizing it," Pepper scoffed. "Who cares about fog? I want to know about Joe and Noreen

McCaffrey. Every woman I spoke with clicked her tongue and shook her head when I mentioned Joe's name, but the second I asked, discreetly, mind you, where he might have stashed Noreen's body, every one of them suddenly had a million things to do."

"I can't imagine why Joe doesn't like you."

"I wasted my time fine-tuning my résumé. There isn't much call for a French interpreter in Murray. And the museums in the valley all seem to revolve around the Rebellion, which is how I would refer to the Civil War if I were you. It's still a sore subject down here, although I'd hold a grudge, too, if my ancestral home had been burned to the ground for no reason. I thought I had the owner of the dress boutique interested in hiring me, but then she asked if I've ever worked in a retail capacity. I couldn't very well lie, could I?" Pepper sighed all over again. "The truth will get you every time."

"We'll figure something out," Lila said.

"I did receive two marriage proposals."

"Only two? It must have been a slow day," Lila said, throwing away a stack of old mail.

"Neither of the men had his teeth in, and you know how I value good oral health."

"And did either of *them* have any idea where Noreen McCaffrey is?"

Pepper dropped so heavily to the old camelback

sofa that dust floated up all around her. Jumping up again in disgust, she said, "It's obvious everyone I've talked to believes Joe did it. What will it take to convince you?"

"Proof?" Lila asked.

Of course, Pepper ignored her. "I should have gone with my first inclination and said I'm a reporter writing a book about Joe and Noreen. Unfortunately, pretending won't bring in an income, and I'm going to need a manicure before too long. By the way, who's that woman talking to Joe?"

This time it was Lila who jumped up. Crowding closer to Pepper at the picture window, she said, "I didn't know she was still here. Her name is Katherine Avery. She's interested in Myrtle Ann's antiques."

"How did she know you were considering selling them?"

"She heard it from someone named Irene—" Lila pronounced it Ah-rene, as Katherine had "—who heard it from a woman named Priscilla, who told Ginny somebody or other, who told Trudy. You remember Trudy, the waitress at the diner?"

Pepper's aristocratic nose flared. "The people of Murray wouldn't tell me anything, but they talked to that woman in linen capris and an old-fashioned hat? How old do you think she is?"

"It's hard to say," Lila answered. "Why?"

"She's pushing forty."

"We're pushing forty," Lila reminded Pepper.

"We're thirty-seven. We won't be pushing forty for two more years. How depressing." Pepper closed her eyes, as if mentally shaking it off. "She didn't waste any time. She must have driven over while I was still asking questions about Joe and getting answers about legendary fog."

"Apparently."

Pepper said, "This situation gets more bizarre every day. What do you make of them?"

Lila wished she knew. Joe and Katherine stood several feet apart, facing each other, backs ramrod-straight. Katherine seemed to be doing most of the talking, a half-grown yellow barn cat making a nuisance of itself wending around her ankles. She finally bent down to pet the creature. When she stood up again, Joe was climbing back on the tractor. Katherine's shoulders drooped as she started for her car.

Lila and Pepper parted like the Red Sea, lest they got caught spying. "How does she know Joe?" Pepper asked from the other side of the heavy drapery.

"He was best man at her wedding."

Pepper's eyebrows arched. "She's married? Hmm."

"A lot of people are married, Pepper."

"She knows something."

"Are you psychic now?"

"You're trying to pick a fight," Pepper said. "That means I'm close to a nerve. It seems we've been going about this all wrong."

"*We* haven't been going about anything," Lila insisted.

"Are you going to consign some of these antiques to her store?"

"I'm considering it."

"Perfect."

Lila was glad she couldn't read minds, because she didn't think she would like what Pepper was thinking. "I don't want you to make trouble for them, Pepper."

"Who's making trouble? What is it you used to say? It's all just the marvelous unfolding of a master plan."

It didn't feel nearly as gratifying to be on the receiving end of her own words of wisdom. Lila didn't doubt that there were forces at work here. Maybe Pepper had been right a few weeks ago when she said Myrtle Ann had brought her into this for a reason. In her mind she pictured ripples on a pond. Was she the stone or the ripples, the unwitting cause or the unsuspecting effect?

"…I would probably have better luck finding a position in a museum in Philadelphia or Boston, but I don't want to leave you here alone with a man suspected of killing his wife."

Pepper was still talking, making Lila wonder how

long she'd zoned out this time. It was happening less often as time went on. She hoped that was a good sign.

"...I don't relish the thought of starving to death. I suppose there's always the world's oldest profession. According to Gwen, that's what I'll have to resort to."

"You've talked to your sister?"

Pepper rolled her eyes. "She called to tell me to stop acting like a spoiled brat and come home. Easy for little Miss Perfect to say. She's fulfilled her family obligation by marrying well and producing two brilliant and mannerly children. I didn't expect her to be supportive, but I really thought Emily would be. As the misunderstood middle child, she sometimes seems to understand what I go through. I haven't heard a peep from her."

Pepper's relationship with her two sisters often made Lila appreciate being an only child. "We're not in such dire straits," Lila said thoughtfully. "Myrtle Ann made a living from the proceeds of a fruit and vegetable stand. Why couldn't we do the same?"

"You mean gardening? As in digging in the dirt?" Pepper wrinkled up her nose.

"You have the option of returning to your grandfather's company. There's still time for you to marry well and produce those mannerly children. My only other option is to go live with my mother and her houseplants."

Just then Pepper's cell phone rang. She was smiling as she checked her caller ID. Putting the phone to her ear, she said, "Emily, I was just talking about you."

Lila watched Pepper's smile slip a notch.

"Why would I do that?" It was a long time before Pepper got another word in edgewise. "What makes you think that?" She began to pace. "Then you're assuming I'll fail, too?" Running her fingers through her short blond hair, she snapped, "How would he know? Is he having me watched?"

Being careful to step over the stacks Lila had made, Pepper quickened her pace and sputtered, "I'll be paranoid if I want to be." She mumbled something very unbecoming then hung up.

"I take it Emily thinks you should do as your grandfather says, too?" Lila asked.

"It's official. They *all* believe I'll fail. Even Emily."

"They're all wrong," Lila said. "Even Emily."

Pepper turned in a huff. "Damn right they're wrong." Extracting her laptop from her bag, she flipped it open. "It's time we put together a plan. What do you have here? Antiques, old letters, goats, chickens and land. Put it all together, and what do you get?"

Lila returned to her sorting and purging while Pepper clicked and muttered under her breath about limitless possibilities. Lila liked the sound of that.

* * *

Joe wasn't discreet about turning his back on Pepper Bartholomew, who was coming toward him along the path. If she wanted him to acknowledge her presence, she was going to have to initiate the conversation.

"You don't like me, do you?" she asked from someplace directly behind him.

He considered his answer while he ran his hand along the bottom of the old rowboat he'd dragged out of the water a few days ago. Checking for weaknesses in the structure, he said, "I don't know you."

"A person doesn't have to know someone to dislike them."

"True. After all, you don't know me."

"Touché."

He hadn't expected such a quick concession. He wondered what she was up to.

"What are you doing?" she asked, easing a little closer.

Wiping epoxy off his hands, he said, "My daughter is coming home for a visit in a few weeks. About the only thing she likes to do out here is row out on the pond. I'm making sure the boat doesn't leak."

He hadn't meant to look at her. The sun cast a golden glow around her blond hair. It wasn't a halo, because she was no angel. She *was* a looker. Not that it mattered. She was one of those women who paid too much for everything. She wore glittery sandals that snapped against the soles of her feet with every step she took. He'd never understood why rich people wore so much black. The last few years before she disappeared, Noreen had taken to doing that.

"What's your daughter's name?"

"Chloe, but you already know that." She was right. He didn't like her. More specifically, he didn't like the way she'd asked everyone he knew about his relationship with Noreen. Like the rest of the world, she assumed he'd killed his wife.

Innocent until proven guilty. What a joke.

He wondered what she was thinking as she stared across the water. Did she know the police had searched the pond shortly after he'd moved here? Did she realize how much dread had filled him at the prospect that they'd find Noreen's body? Or how much dread filled him to think they might never find her?

"What day is today?" she asked.

"Sunday."

"That explains it."

He waited. And waited. Satisfied that the wooden rowboat was in good condition, he tipped it right-side up before giving in and asking, "That explains what?"

"The Sunday quiet. That's what Lila calls this

kind of silence. You're not much of a conversation-alist, are you?"

He'd learned the hard way not to say anything, because taken out of context, *hello* could be damning. Letting her think whatever she wanted, he concentrated on the sweat running down the side of his neck and the view. A hawk glided high above the orchard and the first insects of the summer buzzed over the pond, bringing minnows to the surface and a bullfrog out of hiding. Somewhere, one of the goats rammed its head into something solid.

"Did Lila tell you she's going to teach the goats manners?" Pepper asked.

"Goats aren't pets. They aren't trainable, and they sure as hell don't have manners."

"What do they have?" she asked while he retrieved his sun-warmed shirt from the forsythia bush and put it on.

"Small brains and thick skulls that don't feel anything when they ram brick walls."

"I know people like that."

He wasn't about to admit that stung. "What did you want to tell me?" he asked.

"See there? I knew you'd realize I didn't walk all the way down here in these shoes to talk about goats. Lila sent me to ask for your help."

"Help doing what?"

"Moving furniture."

He wondered why the hell she hadn't said so in the first place. "When?"

"Whenever you're ready."

She left him with a stare he couldn't decipher.

He was dragging the rowboat toward the pond when she called, "By the way—Joe?"

He stopped what he was doing to look at her.

"Heath and Katherine Avery are going to help, too. Lila made me promise I'd tell you that. She's very astute, isn't she? Personally, I wouldn't have been so concerned with your feelings—after all, all we're doing is loading furniture—but a promise is a promise."

This time Joe waited to make sure Pepper actually left before he put the boat in the water. He tied both ends to the dock and added the oars and life preserver. All he had left to do was decide whether to go up to the big house to help move furniture or start walking in the opposite direction and never stop.

CHAPTER 6

Joe shoved the antique dresser against the wall in the cabin's spare room with more force than was necessary. It had been Katherine's idea to move it out here. "For Chloe's sake," she'd said, as if it hadn't been more than two years since she'd told him what he should and shouldn't do where his daughter was concerned.

Last summer Chloe had stayed here the two weeks she'd visited. They'd gotten by without the extra dresser and bed. Not that she'd enjoyed her stay. Joe wasn't fool enough to believe it had anything to do with the furnishings.

"This old trunk is the last of it," Rusty Streeter said, coming in behind him.

Joe arranged the bed so he could walk around it. By the time he turned around, Rusty was gone. The kid would have been a natural at stealing bases, but his childhood hadn't included organized sports. He was quiet and hardworking, too quiet and too hard-working, hell-bent on being invisible in a town that saw everything.

It would have been easier to let him walk back to the big house, but Joe hadn't taken the coward's way out two years ago and he didn't take it now. "Hey, Rusty. Wait up. I'll give you a lift."

Rusty climbed into the passenger seat without questioning Joe's motives.

"Are the Averys paying you for your help?" Joe asked after starting his truck. Not that it was any of his business, but he'd grown up in Murray, and some things rubbed off.

"Yeah. School's almost out. I'm looking for a full-time job for the summer."

"I want to talk to you about that."

The boy shot ahead in his seat, a volcano on the verge of erupting. "I won't let another job get in the way of my job at McCaffrey's. I swear."

"I'm not worried about your job performance," Joe said as the truck bounced over the bumpy lane. "Mc-Caffrey's has never been cleaner. That's not what I wanted to talk to you about."

From the corner of his eye, he could see Rusty begin to relax. Up ahead, Lila, Pepper, Katherine and Heath, the mayor of Murray, were waiting in the shade. It didn't look as if Joe would be relaxing anytime soon.

"Lila wants to turn this place into a vegetable farm. I'm going to need help with that. We'd have to hurry to get the soil worked up and everything planted before it's too late. Do you want the job, or do you want to think about it for a day or two, maybe find something easier?"

"I want the job. Do you know anything about growing vegetables?" the boy asked, looking straight ahead.

"I know about baseball and Bacardi. I only heard about Lila's new plan for the place twenty-five minutes ago."

"It's a pretty good idea," Rusty said thoughtfully. "She's not bad for a Yankee. I think Miz Avery likes her. The missus doesn't seem to have much use for the mayor, though."

"What makes you say that?"

"Look at 'em," Rusty said. "There's enough room between 'em to pitch a cat through."

Joe would have liked to lay his hand on the boy's shoulder and say something reassuring about the way adults behaved, but Rusty shrank away from open displays of affection. There used to be rumors that Bud pounded on his three boys whenever he felt like it. Every few years Social Services got called in, and the rumors stopped for a while. Joe hadn't heard of any abuse since Rusty had gotten taller than Bud.

There was one thing he'd noticed about life. If he looked, he could always find somebody who had it worse than he did. It wasn't a comforting thought. "When's your last day of school?"

"This coming Wednesday."

"I'll plan on you starting bright and early Thursday morning then."

The boy nodded, the movement at the corners of his mouth as close as he ever came to smiling. He got out when Joe brought the truck to a stop. Joe did the same, but a little more slowly and far more reluctantly.

He rested his forearms on the box of his pickup, and surveyed the work waiting to be done in the fields surrounding the house. He'd made a fair amount of progress these past three weeks. The tall weeds had been mowed down, the fences mended, fallen limbs cut into manageable pieces and stacked neatly between the driveway and the road. He'd dragged three junk cars from their hiding places beneath vines and weeds. A man from Fishers Hill was coming to haul them away later in the week. The proceeds from the sale of that firewood and scrap metal would tide Lila over for a while.

On the other side of the driveway, Heath said, "The sooner we get going the sooner Rusty and I will get these antiques unloaded again. Isn't that right, Rusty?"

Joe turned around in time to see Heath's gaze slide over him. With his shirt sweat-stained and the knees of his old jeans dirty, he looked more like he had before he became the mayor of Murray. He didn't look any happier about this little reunion than Joe was.

After a few more tense moments, Rusty and the Averys got in the truck. Nobody moved until after they drove away.

"When you get a minute," Joe said to Lila, "there's something I want to talk to you about."

"If your offer of a drink on the house is still good, I'll stop by McCaffrey's a little later."

It sounded like as good a plan as any to him.

McCaffrey's was all but deserted when Lila arrived late Sunday afternoon. The baseball game was droning from the TV on a shelf behind the bar. She didn't know the man sitting on the bar stool at the far end, but it seemed to her he'd been sitting in the same spot the first time she'd come here with Pepper shortly after they'd arrived in Murray.

"Is Joe here?" she asked.

He looked her up and down as if he thought it was some kind of right. She knew his type. He was one of those men who liked a woman to know her place. Great.

He patted the bar stool next to him and said, "Take a load off, sweetheart. Name's Bud. I won't bite unless you want me to." He waited a full five seconds before laughing out loud.

Lila kept a clear path between her and the door.

"You figure out where Noreen is yet?" When she didn't answer, he said, "What's the matter? Ain't I good enough to talk to? You women are all alike."

"In what way?" she asked.

Where was Joe?

"In every way. Did you bring your crystal ball and Ouija board? My old lady believed in that hocus pocus. What a crock."

"You're married?"

"Was. Me and Joe got us something in common."

"And what's that?" she asked.

"We both married whores. Ain't that right, J.J.?"

Just then Joe shouldered through the doorway, a heavy-looking carton in his arms. Lila had never been so relieved to see someone in her life.

Joe took a moment to refill Bud's glass. Picking up the carton again, he motioned to Lila. "If you don't mind talking while I work, come on back."

Mind? Anything was favorable to continuing the conversation with his only customer.

A narrow hallway led to a back room being used for storage. There were bars on the windows, metal shelves lining the walls and a bare bulb hanging from the low ceiling. Even with the back door open, the room smelled dank. She'd watched old footage of Joe on the pitcher's mound, with the sun in his eyes and fans chanting his name. Although his work at The

Meadows was far less newsworthy, he seemed more suited to the wind and wide open spaces than to a life in this bar. She wondered how he tolerated it. He could have started over anywhere, and yet he'd stayed in Murray. Why?

He slid two fingers into the front pocket of his jeans, brought out a red Swiss Army knife, opened it, and ran it through the top of the cardboard box. "I didn't expect Pepper to let you come alone."

Following the course of that blade, she said, "I didn't give her a choice. I must admit, until you showed up, I was wishing I'd listened to her. You wanted to talk to me about something?"

He answered without looking up. "I hired Rusty Streeter to help at The Meadows."

"You shouldn't have done that, Joe."

"He works hard and cheap." There was an edge in his voice.

At least they were even in that area, because she felt edgy, too, as she said, "I don't doubt that for a minute, but I can't afford to pay him."

"I'll pay him."

"Over my d—"

The pocket knife clattered to the cement floor. They both stared at it, but Joe picked it up, folded it carefully, and returned it to his pocket.

"I didn't mean to imply—"

"That you think I did it, too?" Anger flickered far back in his eyes.

"Actually, I don't believe you did." The subtle shifting of his expression made her glad she'd finally brought it out into the open. "But that doesn't change the fact that I can't take your money."

He returned to his task of arranging whiskey bottles on shelves. "Bud Streeter drinks his paychecks. Feeding the family falls to Rusty."

"Bud? That repulsive man drinking alone at the bar out there is Rusty Streeter's father?"

"I don't know where the kid came by his pride, but he won't take money he hasn't earned. He needs the work, and we need the help."

It always amazed her the way the world carried on no matter what was happening in it. How could a fifteen-year-old boy have to work to feed his siblings in this day and age? Taking a moment to accept the inevitable, she released a loud breath. "In that case, I don't see what choice I have."

"Maybe we could work out a trade," he said.

There was a stillness in the room she hadn't noticed before. Despite the temperature and humidity, she shivered. "What do I have to trade?" she asked very quietly.

"Noreen couldn't have disappeared off the face of the planet without a trace."

"You want me to help you find Noreen?"

His nod sent a second series of shivers up and down her spine. "My venture into police work ended badly, Joe. I haven't had a vision since October. I couldn't even find a lost dog anymore."

"Are you sure about that?"

"It's not something I would fail to notice." Nor did she fail to notice how much effort he put into putting a little distance between them. "Do you still love her?"

Something glittered in his eyes again. Anger? Pain? Surprise? All of the above? She was in over her head here. Feeling color creeping up her neck, she closed her eyes and took a deep breath. She used to be eloquent and witty, never blurting things best left unsaid. She wondered if she would ever be that woman again. "I should be going."

"That alley opens onto Maple Street. Take a left at the corner and you'll be back on Rebellion. It'll save you from having to walk past Bud."

Nothing had been resolved, and yet he was letting it go, relieving her from his suggestion and releasing her from the conversation. She glanced at him before saying, "I'll see you tomorrow, Joe."

Joe told himself he followed Lila into the alley because he needed a breath of fresh air. He was a lousy liar. He wondered if she knew her dress was semitransparent in this light. The color of fresh cream, the skirt swirled around her knees in the slight breeze.

From behind him came the sound of distant laughter. He looked around, because it sounded like Myrtle Ann's cackle, and it raised the hair on the back of his neck. "Did you hear something?" he asked.

She turned around, listened, and shook her head. Of course she hadn't heard anything. They were the only two people in the alley.

She didn't appear to be in a hurry. Despite the fact that she wasn't very tall, she wore sandals with low heels. What relevance that had to anything, he didn't know, except he liked that about her, liked the fact that she didn't put on airs or make demands. She stuck to the basics. And she didn't believe he'd killed Noreen. He wanted to ask her what had brought her to that conclusion. He wanted to ask her to say it again. But he didn't. Once was enough.

She was still looking at him, the wind still toying with her hair and dress. And he wanted—

God help him, he wanted closure and answers. And peace. He wanted that most of all.

"What would you say if I told you I never loved her?" Where the hell had that come from?

She came partway back to him. Lowering her voice, she said, "I would tell you I used to hear that a lot from the couples I counseled. In your case, I wouldn't recommend mentioning it to anyone else."

He didn't tell her he would take it under advisement, because it didn't matter. He'd never needed to tell anyone how he'd felt about his wife. Somehow, they'd known. There weren't many secrets in Murray. But there was one. Waiting to go back inside until after Lila disappeared from view around the corner, he thought, make that two.

At dusk, Katherine loaded the dishwasher and started it. Staring out the window at the still backyard, she listened to the sounds carrying through the house. A television droned in Heath's study. It didn't completely cover the quiet that was her life these days.

Footsteps padded behind her, followed by the slight rustle of papers. She knew without looking that Heath had finished reading the newspaper in the study and had brought it to the kitchen table. He'd always been conscientious that way. She used to feel so lucky when her friends complained about their husbands' slovenly habits. To this day Heath knew how to work the toilet seat and the dishwasher. He knew as well as she did which fork to use. They both said please and thank you. As the mayor and his wife, they attended luncheons, meetings, banquets, fundraisers and church socials. Even when they were home alone, they were courteous and polite. Over supper tonight, they'd discussed local politics and the problems with the new mileage proposal. They never argued. They never made up, either.

She closed her mind to the thought.

Sensing that he was still in the room, she finally faced him. He'd washed up and changed his clothes after helping the oldest Streeter boy carry all those wonderful antiques into the store. Heath looked as good in beige chinos as he had in faded jeans. The first time Katherine had taken him home eighteen years ago, her mama had taken her aside and said, "That boy cleans up well. I wouldn't let this one get away if I were you."

She'd been picky about the men she dated, but she'd had no intention of letting him get away. His hair was still as black as coal. She could always tell when it was time for a haircut because, like tonight, it curled around his forehead. She used to love running her fingers through those curls. The memory brought a sharp sense of loss of something precious. "Did you need something?" she asked.

Perhaps he felt the loss, too, or maybe he just wanted the uncomfortable silence to be over, because he finally said, "I have a nine o'clock meeting with the board tomorrow morning."

Instantly, she understood what he was asking. "I picked up your dark suit at the dry cleaner's yesterday. Your light-blue tie goes so nicely with your eyes."

He didn't question her taste or how she'd known what he needed. She suspected that he would have remained in the kitchen if she'd given him any encouragement whatsoever, but she didn't, and he returned to the study as quietly as he always did.

Rather than dwell on the lump in her throat, she found something constructive to do. She paid some bills and leafed through a magazine, clipping a recipe for sweet potato casserole—why on earth she needed another one, she didn't know, since she already had dozens of them. After filing it in the recipe box she rarely used anymore, she read an article about antique furniture and checked the newspaper for estate sales. At ten o'clock, she took a long shower. As she did every night, she wrapped her robe securely around her and tied the sash tight before venturing out to make sure the doors and windows were locked.

Heath waited to turn off the television until she'd passed by the doorway of the study. As he always did, he took his shower after she'd vacated the bathroom. The system worked well, giving her enough time to apply her lotion and turn down the bed and get in on her side, and giving both of them enough time to pretend she was asleep when he came to bed.

It hadn't always been this way. They used to talk about anything and everything. They used to laugh. She tried not to think about what else they used to do.

It wasn't as if either of them wanted to live this way. They'd tried to rekindle what they'd once had. Eventually, going through the motions became more difficult than pretending they were both content.

She sighed. She'd been doing that a lot these past few days.

Moonlight slanted through the window, the silver beams stretching all the way to the bed. It was all she could do to keep from reaching out and touching a moon shadow with the tip of one finger. Did the moon have anything to do with her melancholy tonight?

The bed dipped as Heath rolled over, his weight jostling her slightly, the momentum drawing the sheet off her shoulder. Ever so carefully, he put it back again, his fingertips so close to her skin she felt the warmth of his hand, if not his touch. She wondered what would happen if she moved the slightest bit, or if, just once, he wasn't quite so careful not to touch her. But she didn't move and he was careful. And as they did every night, they settled on their respective sides, two people facing outward instead of in.

She lay awake long after his breathing became slow and rhythmic, thinking about their life together.

He would undoubtedly be the most handsome man at that meeting in the morning. And the most rested.

From deep inside her came a yearning to break out of this silent, suffocating rut. She wasn't sure how. She only knew she didn't want to go on this way.

It had taken all her courage to pay Lila Delaney a visit the first time. Despite the nerves clamoring in the pit of her stomach, something had been trying to come to life inside her ever since. She didn't understand what it all meant, but she'd taken the first step the other day when she'd knocked on Lila's door. Today, she'd taken the second, and she didn't think she had it in her to turn back now.

Dear God, she hoped not.

CHAPTER 7

Was that a knock on the door?

Deciding it was just more of the crashing and banging coming from the kitchen where Pepper was engaged in a battle of wills with the ice cubes she was attempting to crush with a hammer, Lila rested her head on the arm of the sofa. But the knock came again, and this time it was accompanied by a voice she recognized.

"Lila? Pepper? Did y'all get the last of those wildflowers planted?"

Sitting up, Lila said, "Yes, we did. Come in, Katherine."

Once inside, Katherine Avery took one look at Lila and practically gasped. "Are you all right?"

The question erased any doubt Lila may have had regarding how she looked this morning. For three days Joe and Rusty had worked beneath the hot sun, turning the ground over with rusty machinery and an old tractor that spewed black smoke into the air, until they were covered in soot and dust and the red soil they worked up was practically powder. Meanwhile, Lila and Pepper had planned the layout and sketched diagrams and carted home flats of flowers and seedlings and packets of vegetable and flower seeds. After Joe and Rusty left each afternoon, the two former Radcliffe girls had sectioned off rows, pounded in stakes and strung lines of garden twine, painstakingly planting every shoot and carefully covering each seed. But Katherine already knew that, for she'd stopped by last night after Joe left for Mc-Caffrey's. Pepper was convinced the timing meant something.

"Aside from a little sunburn and fatigue, I'm fine," Lila said. It was true. A few months ago she'd been physically and emotionally drained and on the verge of collapse. The process of organizing the house and planting the meadows had the opposite effect on her. "I'm glad you came by. I wanted to show you this."

Katherine took the sheet of yellowed stationary from Lila's outstretched hand. "Where did you find this?"

"In a drawer in the dining room," Lila said, reading over Katherine's shoulder.

June 1897.
1. Bilt fire in backyard. Set tubs so smoke wont blow in eyes if wind is pert
2. Make piles, 1 pile white, 1 pile colored, 1 pile work britches and rags.

3. Shave one hole cake lie soap into bilin water.

4. To make starch, stir flour in cool water. Thin with bilin water.

5. Scrub whites hard on board, then bile. Rub colored, don't bile.

6. Take things out with broomstick handle, then rinch and starch.

7. Hang old rags on fence. Spread tea towels on grass.

8. Pour rinch water in flower bed.

9. Scrub porch with leftover soapy water then turn tubs upside down.

10. Go put on clean dress, smooth hair with combs. Brew cup of tea and sit on a rock to count yer blessings. How fortunate we are to have all that we have.

"What do you think?" Lila asked.

"These handwritten instructions were once passed from generation to generation," Katherine said, "but I've never actually seen one. I think this could be worth something, if you're willing to part with it."

"Oh, I'm willing," Lila said.

"Who are you talking to?" Pepper called on the way to the living room.

"Look who's here *this morning*," Lila said, her eyes adding, *so much for your theory*.

Pepper's eyebrows arched thoughtfully, but before she could comment, the door burst open and anything not battened down shook beneath the on-rushing stampede as two young boys raced inside. "Ricky's gotta use the toilet," the older of the two said. "And it ain't the kind he can do behind the barn."

Lila and Pepper were speechless. Thankfully, Katherine seemed to know what to do. "Normally," she said, "we make introductions first. In the future, you'll say 'May I.' But in this instance, come with me."

The older child remained in the dining room, torn between fear and duty.

"Who are you?" Pepper asked.

"Ryan Matthew Streeter. I'm eleven years old. Ricky's eight. Rusty told me to keep an eye on 'im and to keep out of your way. Tell Ricky I'm waitin' for him outside."

An instant later the door slammed.

In the ensuing silence, Pepper declared, "I have never understood what people find so adorable about children. What do you make of Katherine?"

"She thinks Myrtle Ann's great-aunt's washing instructions could be worth something. See for yourself," she said, offering Pepper a look at the paper in her hand. "We don't have it so bad."

"Tell that to my throbbing thumb. Here. Try a sip of this, and then try answering my question."

Lila sniffed the drink. Recognizing the strong scent of bourbon, she said, "I don't know what to make of her. But I like her. What is this?"

"Mint julep."

"Since when do you drink mint juleps? And isn't it a little early in the day?" As if to prove Lila's point, Louie the rooster crowed outside the living room window.

"When in Rome." Pepper lowered stiffly to the other end of the sofa and began to read. "Besides," she said when she'd finished, "the French call this *L'heure bleue*."

"That dark hour between night and dawn," Katherine said softly on her way back into the room, causing Lila and Pepper to start guiltily.

"It's ten o'clock in the morning," Lila reminded them both.

"Not in France, it's not," Katherine said. "If it's all right with you, Lila, I would like to take those instructions home with me. I think I could auction them off on eBay. I'll photograph this, and perhaps put together a little collection to pique bidders' interest."

The toilet flushed in another part of the house. Pipes rattled, and then the little boy was making a mad dash for the door.

"Not so fast!" Katherine's voice stopped him in his tracks. "What do you say to Miz Delaney?"

Interestingly, he knew which one was Lila. "I went poo," he told her. At Katherine's stricken look, he added, "And I washed my hands after."

He raced outside and slammed the door behind him. It seemed to be a family trait.

"I take it you know him?" Pepper asked.

"He's Bud Streeter's boy."

Lila said, "Joe mentioned there were younger brothers, but I didn't realize Rusty was bringing them with him."

"Obviously, Joe knows they're here," Pepper said, casually handing the tankard to Katherine. "What do you think about Joe?"

"What do *you* think about him?" Katherine sampled the icy drink.

"Do you think he did it?"

Lila had to close her gaping mouth, but Katherine calmly handed the tankard back to Pepper and said, "Lordy, I hope not."

Pepper and Lila exchanged a glance, because that wasn't an answer. Measuring the weight of the nearly empty tankard, Pepper said, "Let me know if you want another *sip*."

Katherine ducked her dark head. Lila was pretty sure she was smiling.

An enigma, Pepper's gaze told Lila.

Definitely.

* * *

"There you are." Lila found Pepper stretched out on the wicker chaise lounge they'd brought down from the attic.

"God, I miss air-conditioning. Even a breeze would be nice. Especially if it was accompanied by a steady rain shower."

"Are you hungry?" Lila asked, putting the platter of sandwiches on the outdoor table.

"Peanut butter again?" Pepper removed her sunglasses and squinted into the distance. "Is that a rain cloud on the horizon?"

It looked like jet emissions to Lila. Pepper had been watching the sky for signs of rain ever since they'd planted the gardens last week. "Don't worry," Lila said. "It'll rain."

"It had better soon or we'll go broke paying those boys a dollar for every row they water."

Pepper put two fingers in her mouth and whistled, and Lila called, "Is anybody hungry?"

The younger boys laid down their watering cans. Joe and Rusty emerged from the barn. All of them washed at the outdoor spigot, and everybody clambered up the porch steps.

Now that Lila had had a chance to interact with the boys, she enjoyed them. The youngest was unkempt, but not homely, and the least shy of the three. Yesterday she'd chuckled at something he'd said. He'd looked up at her as if he'd never seen a woman laugh. It made her want to laugh more.

This was the third time Rusty had brought his brothers with him. Lila didn't know what alternative arrangements were made on the days they didn't accompany him to The Meadows. When they came, she fed them, all of them, including Joe.

Normally he dug in as eagerly as the kids. Today, his sandwich remained suspended between his paper plate and his mouth, his gaze on the car pulling into the driveway.

"Am I too late?" Katherine called, hauling a heavy-looking basket with her to the porch.

"Too late for what?" Lila asked, helping Katherine with the basket.

"For dinner of course." Katherine glanced at Joe first, and then the boys. "I fixed y'all a little something to eat. I hope you like sweet potato casserole and catfish poorboys and grits."

Nobody seemed interested in peanut butter all of a sudden.

The next thing Lila knew they were all inside. The dining room table was opened up, leaves added, places set with real dishes and cutlery and glasses. Katherine served from the far end of the table, passing each plate to the right. She didn't take a seat at the place Lila had set for her.

"Aren't you joining us?" Lila asked.

Again, Katherine glanced at Joe. If tension were food, she could have dished that up with the fish. "Perhaps another time."

"If you're sure I can't change your mind, I'll walk you out," Lila said.

"That isn't necessary."

"Neither was all this. It smells delicious, by the way."

Katherine had reached the doorway when Joe said, "If you come tomorrow, Katherine, you might as well allow yourself enough time to eat with us."

She glanced over her shoulder at him. In fact, everyone was looking from Joe to Katherine and back again. Lila felt as if she were watching a foreign film without subtitles. She was still trying to interpret the silent exchange when Katherine nodded. Lila didn't know what had been settled, but something had. Joe picked up his fork. One by one, the kids did the same.

Pepper's eyes were saucers. Lila imagined hers were, too, as they followed Katherine to her car.

"It's not what y'all are thinking."

"You know what we're thinking?" Pepper asked. "Are you psychic?"

"All women become slightly psychic eventually."

"Meaning you are?" Pepper asked.

"Other than the usual women's intuition and those pesky occasional unexplainable goose bumps, no. Not the way Lila and Myrtle Ann were."

"Myrtle Ann was psychic?" Lila asked, shading her eyes with her hand.

Katherine had reached her car, but she made no move to get in. "You don't think Myrtle Ann brought you here for nothing, do you?"

"I tried to tell her," Pepper declared. "But enough about that. What did you think *we'all* were thinking?"

"Why did she bring me here?" Lila asked, stepping in front of Pepper. "I've lost my intuitive abilities."

"Are you sure?" Katherine asked.

"Joe asked me the same thing."

"He did?" Katherine said.

"When?" Pepper quipped at the same time.

"Last Sunday when I went to McCaffrey's. He wants me to help him find Noreen."

"Are you going to?" Katherine asked.

"You're not going to!" Pepper exclaimed. Again, they'd spoken at the same time.

Lila considered both statements, and then she considered both women. "I'm thinking about it. Are you planning to join us for dinner tomorrow, Katherine?"

Katherine slid into the driver's seat and closed the door. "I'm thinking about it," she said just before she drove away.

* * *

Guessing what Katherine would bring for dinner had become a favorite pastime for everyone at The Meadows this week. Would it be ribs and collard greens or curried scallops and custard pie, scalloped corn and crab cakes or okra skillet and pecan bars? Today, second and third helpings of fried chicken and wedding potatoes had disappeared in record time. With the boys' mouths full, keeping up any semblance of conversation had fallen to the adults, or more accurately, to Lila, Pepper and Katherine. Joe barely said a word.

Dinner, as lunch was called around here, was over now, and the dishes, practically licked clean, were stacked in the steamy kitchen. Joe and Rusty were hoeing in the gardens, and Ricky and Ryan were playing inside Myrtle Ann's old Corvair while Lila, Pepper and Katherine finished a glass of sweetened iced tea on the porch.

"How well did you know Noreen?" Pepper asked.

"How well does anyone know anybody?"

The porch swing creaked as Lila swayed in it, the breeze as elusive as Katherine's answer. Interestingly, all personal information hadn't been completely unforthcoming. For instance, she'd told Lila and Pepper about the car accident that had taken her mother and father five years ago. She also mentioned that she and the mayor had been married for eighteen years. What they didn't know was why Katherine had stared into the distance—where Joe happened to be working—when she'd supplied the information.

"What about you two?" Katherine asked. "Neither of you ever married?"

Fanning herself with a magazine, Pepper said, "Believe me, I never dreamed I would be thirty-seven and still single. I was so positive I would be divorced by now."

Katherine laughed, but Lila said, "I was engaged for five years. You could say it ended badly."

Letting the condensation on her glass cool the skin exposed where her tank top dipped low, Pepper said, "Discovering your fiancé having toe-curling sex on national television takes ending badly to a new level."

"Thanks for that quaint mental picture. It really jogged my memory."

Pepper blew Lila a kiss.

"Five years is a long time to be engaged," Katherine said, fingering the purple ribbon on the straw hat lying in the chair next to her. "Was the wedding being planned?"

Lila shook her head.

And Katherine said, "Your instincts must have been trying to tell you something. Do you miss him?"

"I miss my instincts more."

"What do you miss?"

Not even Pepper or Lila's mother had asked her this. "I miss closing my eyes and going on that momentary ride through the universe. And I miss opening them again and knowing, just knowing the answer to whatever I'd been unsure of."

"So that's how you did it?" Katherine asked. "You closed your eyes and let it happen?"

Pepper said, "The first time I saw her in action was just before chemistry class our freshman year. Professor Lundstrom was notorious for throwing pop quizzes. Old Lundo lived to fail as many students as humanly possible. That day, Lila alerted us to his plans, and we all went to class prepared."

"I'll bet that cooked his goose," Katherine said.

"You took the words right out of my mouth," Pepper said dryly.

"What else do you remember?" Katherine said to Lila.

"When I was seven years old I told my mother the house on the corner was on fire."

"Was it?"

"It burned down the next day."

"Was your mother concerned about your gift?"

"My mother was concerned if I didn't wear three sweaters, or if I didn't get eight hours of sleep every night or eat a good breakfast or get straight As, but my intuition never bothered her. In fact, she nurtured it."

"You'd have to know Rose," Pepper explained. "She kept Lila in white candles, and was always trying to get her to tell her the winning lottery numbers. Actually, we're going to need a winning lottery ticket if it doesn't rain soon."

"You use white candles?" Katherine asked.

"White candles and moonlight were part of the celebration afterwards. I remember the first time my mother suggested we celebrate that way. Amanda Kelsey's dog had gone missing. I was nine years old and Amanda was eleven, and beautiful. She had all her permanent teeth and was already wearing a bra. She promised she would repay me with her undying gratitude and be my best friend for life if I led her to poor Bitsy."

"And did you?" Katherine asked.

"We found poor Bitsy cooling off in the Burkes' wading pool three blocks away. That night my mother lit white candles out on the patio and we danced in the moonlight."

"And the girl with the permanent teeth, training bra and promise of undying friendship and devotion?"

Lila shrugged. "She never spoke to me again."

"God, those were the days." Dodging the flip-flop Lila threw at her, Pepper said, "Is that a rain cloud on the horizon?"

Lila and Katherine didn't even bother looking.

"Getting back to your intuition," Katherine said gently.

"I was slightly psychic," Lila said. "It was how I defined myself."

"You weren't slightly anything," Pepper declared. "You were incredible." Noticing Lila and Katherine looking at her, she said, "What I meant was you *are* incredible, present tense all the way. I'm not helping, am I? Okay, Katherine, take it away."

Ice cubes jangled in Katherine's glass as she said, "Remember when you told me the woman I thought I would be by now is inside me, waiting for me to recognize her and reconnect? Maybe the same holds true for you. Close your eyes."

After a little more prodding, Lila did as she was told.

"What do you hear?" Katherine asked.

One of the goats butted a fence post. Birds twittered. That jet she'd noticed broke the sound barrier, but other than that, she heard nothing, saw nothing, felt nothing. Opening her eyes again, she said, "It's no use."

"You're in the south now, missy and that attitude just won't do."

Lila hadn't been scolded in years, but she closed her eyes and tried again.

"Lila, you don't have t—"

Katherine must have silenced Pepper. "Now I

want you to concentrate. Feel the breeze on your arms and face."

"There's a breeze?"

This time Katherine shushed Pepper out loud before saying, "Listen to the flutter of gnats. They're said to sound like angels' wings. Smell the moist red soil."

"Moist?" Pepper asked. "All right already. I'm shushing."

Lila took a deep breath and inhaled one of those gnats. Waiting for her to recover from the subsequent coughing spell, Katherine said, "Smell the moist red soil, the same soil the Native Americans smelled five hundred years ago."

Lila's eyes teared up, because she felt honored to be smelling soil Native Americans had smelled five hundred years ago, even if it wasn't moist.

"Do you hear it?" Katherine whispered.

Lila listened, barely breathing.

"It's the earth breathing," Katherine said. "You haven't lost the magic. You just have to find another way to let it out, or in, depending upon how it works for you."

Her eyes closed tight, her heart beating steadily, Lila lost track of time. She could hear the sounds of summer, the scrape of a hoe, a distant airplane, the creak of the porch swing, and if she listened hard enough, she heard the slight breeze rustling the leaves on the magnolia tree next to the porch. Although those sounds didn't raise goose bumps on her arms or create a vibration against her skin, she felt rejuvenated somehow.

"I think you might be on to something," she whispered.

Silence.

"Katherine?" She opened one eye. "Pepper?" She opened the other.

Lila was alone on the porch. Pepper was strolling toward the orchard, her cell phone to her ear, and Katherine was starting her car.

"That was a sneaky way of getting out of doing the dishes, both of you!" She thought she heard Pepper laugh and Katherine sigh.

But it might have been the earth breathing.

CHAPTER 8

"Watch it, Joe."

Joe jumped out of the imaginary path of an old car on blocks. Bending down slightly in order to look at the two boys playing inside, he said, "Do you have a license to drive that thing?"

"Don't need no license." Ryan Streeter oversteered while his little brother made engine noises from the tattered seat next to him.

Joe was on his way back to the cabin to get cleaned up before taking his shift at the bar, but he changed course and made a show of looking the vehicle over. "What's she got under the hood?"

"A hemmy," eleven-year-old Ryan said, as if it should have been obvious.

Myrtle Ann's old Corvair hadn't been driven in almost twenty years. It had sat for so long its engine belts had rotted. Mice had made nests in the oil pan and radiator, and bees had made their home in the exhaust pipe. One wheel was missing entirely, the other tires as flat as pancakes. It was in sorry shape, and the plan had been to sell it for scrap along with the other two rust heaps he'd uncovered.

Evidently Lila had seen Rusty admiring the car. When Gabe Pattison came to pick up the old automobiles, she'd told him to take the Buicks but leave the Corvair. Joe had been there when she'd given it to Rusty. He was pretty sure Rusty was in love, with Lila or the car, maybe both.

Men had an unexplainable fascination with cars. It started young. Ryan and Ricky already had the bug. Maybe that was why Joe stuck out his thumb and played along.

Instantly, there was a horrendous screeching of pretend brakes. "Where to, mister?" Ricky called through the missing windshield.

"Depends. Where are you headed?" Joe asked.

"Anyplace that ain't here," Ryan said, almost too serious to be playing.

"In that case, you're going my way." Joe glanced into the backseat, his gaze once again inexplicably drawn there for a moment before he hopped on a pretend running board and held on to the cracked mirror.

The sound effects were convincing. Tires squealed and corners were taken as if on rails. One minute they were being chased by the police, the next by gangsters. The boys' faces were flushed as if the wind actually was coursing over them. They each wore one of Joe's old baseball caps that made their ears stick out. It was a wonder either of them could see out from beneath the bill.

"Look out for that goat!" Ricky yelled.

"Eat my dust," Ryan shouted.

The goat watched from behind the fence, lazily chewing an old shoe.

Ryan and Ricky Streeter looked like normal kids lost in make-believe. Maybe that was what they were. Maybe in play, their home life didn't exist. The boys were resilient. Joe wondered if the same held true for girls, his girl especially.

Ryan spun the wheel and Ricky let loose a simulated screech of tires. "End of the line, mister."

Joe hopped off. "Thanks for the lift, boys." He glanced into the backseat again. "Ladies." He tugged at the bill of his ball cap and nodded at the two women who hadn't said a word, his gaze resting a little longer on a pair of hazel eyes all over again.

He and Lila hadn't had an opportunity to speak much the last few days. It seemed someone was always coming or going around here. Pepper had put up signs around town advertising camp wood. Either there were an unbelievable number of campers in the valley all of a sudden, or folks were curious about the new owner of The Meadows. Word had spread that Lila was selling more antiques, too. And Katherine brought dinner every day now. He didn't know what Lila did in her spare time. A few days ago she'd discovered ten gallons of perfectly good paint in the basement.

"Was Myrtle Ann planning to have the house painted?" she'd asked.

Joe was more inclined to believe she hadn't been able to pass up a good sale, but what difference did it make? So he'd shrugged and said, "Could be."

Lila had looked at him. "Would you and Rusty be willing to paint the house?"

He was the first to admit that scraping paint, especially on a house the size of this one, wasn't something he would enjoy. He'd told her he would do it, though, and then he'd told her she was being very generous to Rusty.

She'd turned those hazel eyes of hers on him and guilelessly said, "Let's see. I coerce you into doing menial labor under horrible conditions and then *you* pay Rusty to help you. I'm not the one being generous, Joe."

In that moment, he'd understood Rusty's infatuation. There was a good chance Joe needed his head examined, although another need moved front and center.

"You gonna stand there all day, mister?" Ricky shouted.

"Hold on to your hat, kid," Pepper complained. "I'm getting out at this stop, too. Are you coming, Lila?"

Lila answered without breaking eye contact with Joe. "I want to go all the way to Topeka."

"Where's Topeka?" Ryan asked.

"It's in Kansas, kid," Pepper said. "Right next to Oz."

The sound effects were getting louder again. Now that Lila was alone in the backseat, Joe had half a mind to climb in next to her. He didn't know what was wrong with him. Okay, he knew. There was something else that manifested early in males, something instinctive and more dangerous than a fascination with cars.

He was going to do his damnedest to outrun it.

"For the love of Christmas, Joe, where's the fire?" Pepper Bartholomew fell into step beside him despite the fact that he hadn't slowed down. "Is that a rain cloud on the horizon?"

"How should I know?"

As usual, she seemed unfazed by his bluntness. "The garden has been in for ten days. I don't know how you people stand relying on Mother Nature." She slapped a hand over her mouth. "My sister Emily's right. I am a snob."

Since he didn't have a clue where she was going with this conversation, he said, "Do you want me to tell you Emily's wrong?"

Flipping her sunglasses from the top of her head onto her nose, she said, "I would rather hear you tell *Emily* that, but that's expecting a great deal, even for me."

It was the middle of June, and the first wildflowers were blooming along the lane between garden plots. "Does it ever cool off around here?" she asked.

"Of course it does. Usually sometime in October."

"Great. Do I see something green?" She darted to the row marker. "We planted zinnias here and pole beans in that row. Do these look like zinnias and pole beans to you?"

He surveyed the carpet of green spreading through the rows. "They're weeds. They're coming up everywhere."

She shook her head. "Why do weeds grow without rain but flowers and vegetables don't?"

"Weeds have been adapting a lot longer."

"I don't think I'm cut out to be a farmer," she said. "Don't tell Lila."

"You don't think she knows?"

"You're probably right." Being mindful of the bees buzzing nearby, she said, "You were hoping she would follow you out here instead of me, weren't you?"

"I'm a married man."

He saw his reflection in her sunglasses. It was a distorted image and reminded him that things weren't always what they seemed.

"Then you think it's possible Noreen is alive?" She slapped her hand over her mouth a second time. "That was unfeeling and uncalled-for."

She was right about that, but the truth of the

matter was, Joe didn't know what to think anymore. "Noreen loved Chloe, at least as much as she could love anybody. I can't believe she would have left willingly without somehow getting word to our daughter."

He walked to the edge of the pond. On the other side, the rowboat bobbed on the water. The way the sky was reflected on the smooth surface made the boat appear to be floating on thin air, which just went to prove that things weren't always what they seemed.

"You didn't do it, did you?"

"No. But you already know that. Otherwise you wouldn't be here." He scooped up a stone and pitched it. Just like that, the sky disappeared and the surface was just water again. "Why are you here?"

"I told you. My grandfather cut off my funding."

"I mean here. Now. Talking to me."

"Lila's been practicing."

"Practicing what?" he asked, skipping a second stone.

"What do you think? Katherine got her started a few days ago. She told Lila to close her eyes and let the magic happen. It seems to me Lila's had her eyes closed a lot since then. One of these days she'll be lighting white candles and dancing in the moonlight while the universe vibrates all around her."

Joe supposed that was another difference between men and women. Women could use words like candles, moonlight and vibrate in the same sentence without thinking about sex.

"Lila said your daughter's coming home soon."

He didn't bother telling her that Chloe didn't consider this home. "I'm driving to Philadelphia to pick her up on Friday."

"This place is getting crowded. How long will you be gone?"

"A few days."

"What's your daughter like?" she asked.

"You'll see."

"You're not an easy man to talk to, you know that?"

"Yes, I know."

Noise erupted in the distant meadow. Ryan Streeter must have discovered the horn. It sounded as if Ricky wanted a turn behind the wheel. Joe could hear them arguing from here.

Shading her eyes with one hand, Pepper said, "Where's their mother?"

"Has anyone ever mentioned that you ask a lot of questions?"

"Isn't that the only way to get answers?"

He'd give her that round. "Bud's wife ran off with another man when Ricky was a baby."

"Who would leave her children with a man like Bud Streeter? Who would *have* children with a man like Bud Streeter? Those kids deserve better."

"I thought you didn't like kids."

She shot him a leveling look. "Riding in the back of that junked car was Lila's idea."

"Who are you trying to convince?"

She shrugged. "Don't tell my grandfather. If he discovers I'm being kind to children, he'll use it to my disadvantage."

Only women like Pepper were afraid of their wealthy grandfathers. Only women like Pepper used terms like "to my disadvantage." Only women like Pepper were nicknamed Pepper.

"I doubt I'll ever meet your grandfather, but if I did, I'd tell him he must be blind if he hasn't seen that side of you for himself."

"I'm tearing up over here. That sounded suspiciously like a compliment."

Joe almost smiled. "I'll be more careful in the future." He released the last stone across the pond. It skipped six times. His record was eight.

"You will be careful, won't you?" she asked.

He wasn't fool enough to believe she was concerned about his trip to Philadelphia. She was worried about Lila. She cared about more than children.

"I'll be careful," he said. And he would be. These last few years, careful had become his middle name.

Katherine heard the rustle of papers behind her. Heath had finished reading his newspaper and had carried it to the kitchen table the way he always did this time of the evening. The last she'd known, it was six-thirty. She had no idea she'd been online so long.

She'd been following her auction on eBay all day. She'd combined those handwritten wash-day instructions with an old washtub, hair combs and a leather diary. The items had photographed well, and yet the initial bid hadn't been raised all afternoon. After supper, things had started picking up.

"What are you doing?"

She jumped two inches off her chair. "Heath. I didn't know you were still in the kitchen."

"I can see that."

Had there been a trace of irritation in his voice? She glanced at him, and quickly dismissed the possibility. Heath Avery didn't get irritated. Cool, calm and collected, he looked exactly the way he always looked at the end of a long day. His shirt was slightly wrinkled, the sleeves rolled up, the top button open, his tie, somewhere.

"What are you doing?" he asked again.

She motioned to the colorful display on her laptop. "I'm following an online auction."

"An antique you're interested in?" he asked.

"Actually, it's a grouping of Myrtle Ann's old things I put together to auction for Lila Delaney."

"You've been spending a lot of time at The Meadows."

There was an awkward stretch of silence while she considered the best way to answer. She pressed her lips together so no sound would escape until she was ready. Imposing an iron control on her own voice, she said, "Joe has asked Lila to help him find Noreen."

The room went utterly still again. Not even the computer made a sound.

"Is she going to?" Heath finally asked.

"I think so."

Her computer beeped, signaling that someone just upped the last bid. The new amount didn't even register in her mind. She was too busy listening to Heath's footsteps as he left the room.

After he'd retreated to his study, Katherine released the breath she hadn't known she was holding, and glanced around her immaculate black-and-white kitchen, at the ceramic rooster she'd searched high and low for, the granite countertops and the stainless steel refrigerator and stove. The color scheme seemed cold now, sterile. Or maybe it was just a reflection of her life.

She was still in her desk chair hours later when Heath returned to the kitchen. "Are you going to get in the shower?"

She glanced out the window, surprised to see that

the sun was down and the moon was out. "I didn't realize it was so late. You go ahead," she told him, allowing herself one glance in his direction.

He hesitated as if surprised that she was altering the routine. "Will you be long?" he asked.

"I don't know. Don't wait up."

"You're sure?"

"I'm sure. Good night, Heath."

His footsteps fell lightly on the stairs. Eventually the shower rumbled overhead. Three more bids had been cast by the time the water was turned off again. Katherine imagined him climbing into that big bed alone.

Let the magic happen, she'd told Lila.

The air conditioner burst on. Surely that was the reason she shivered.

Silence settled into the lonely house. Silent and lonely. That was her life these days.

She fixed herself a cup of herbal tea. At midnight she looked out the kitchen window at the still backyard where the children she'd once wanted had never played. The moon was full and bright now, a white orb in the indigo sky. Intellectually, she knew moonlight was really simply the reflection of sunlight off the moon's surface. But something happened to the rays in the refraction, turning them from yellow to silver. Tonight, those silver moonbeams reached through the maple tree, casting shadows, like crooked fingers, on the lawn.

Yearning swelled behind her breastbone, so intense it was painful. She knew what she wanted. Was it futile?

What was she hoping to accomplish? Or did she have something to prove? What could she prove? That she was too young to feel this old?

She was forty, and she wanted moonlight. She wanted candlelight. She wanted magic.

She returned to the chair and clicked on the auction once again. Her eyes opened wider. "Well, well, well," she whispered to herself.

She hopped to her feet and jitterbugged across the kitchen. Feeling silly and self-conscious, she stopped and glanced around to make sure no one was watching. Years ago she and Heath had taken dance lessons, but her love of dancing had begun long before that. How long had it been since she'd danced?

"Call me sentimental." She did a fun little two-step out of spite. "Call me crazy." She switched to the "YMCA," which led directly into the "Macarena" and a quiet little giggle. "Call me tomorrow, call me a cab, call me a fool, but call me."

Okay, she was dancing alone and talking to herself. Worse, she wasn't making any sense. She looked around the kitchen again. Why did she expect everything to make sense all the time?

Her gaze fell upon her car keys.

What she wanted to do was a little crazy and completely sentimental and maybe even a little wild. It didn't make perfect sense. *All the better reason to do it.*

Feeling giddy, she scribbled a note for Heath, just in case he came looking for her, not that he would. She grabbed her keys and let herself out before she could change her mind.

"Unless somebody's dead or dying, go away!" Pepper peeked out the window. "On second thought, go away anyway."

The knocking only increased. "Pepper. Your light's on. Unless you're walking and talking in your sleep, I know you're awake."

Didn't Katherine Avery ever sleep?

Pepper flipped the lock and Katherine breezed in. "'All things by immortal power, near of far, to each other linked are, that thou canst not stir a flower without troubling of a star.'"

"It takes more than the ability to quote Francis Thompson to impress me," Pepper grumbled. "What are you doing here?"

"I knew you'd be up."

Katherine's cheeks were flushed, her eyes lively. Pepper had never seen her this way.

"Night used to be my favorite time of the day."

"Mine, too," Pepper said. "What does that have to do with any—"

"There's a silence about the night that doesn't exist any other time," Katherine said. "Tonight I realized I've been wasting it sleeping."

"Are you drunk?"

"Not yet. Do you have that tankard of mint julep left?" Katherine asked.

"As a matter of fact, I do, but—"

"Good. Say all you want about white candles and moonlight, but a true southern celebration isn't complete without some form of sour mash whiskey."

Pepper glanced down at her silk tank and boxers. She'd fallen asleep in front of the TV, but she was awake now. And admittedly she was getting into the spirit. "I'm not dressed for a celebration."

"It's come as you are."

Eyeing Katherine's pale blue lounging pants, Pepper asked, "What exactly are we celebrating?"

"Is Lila asleep?" Katherine asked. "If she is, wake her up. She needs to be in on this."

It turned out they didn't need to wake Lila. The commotion had taken care of that. She padded into the room while Pepper was pouring icy liquid into glasses. Her hair was mussed, her feet bare, a white nightgown suspended loosely from satin ribbons at her shoulders. "What's going on?" Lila asked. "Katherine? What are you doing here?" She squinted at the clock on the stove. "What time is it?"

"Evidently some sort of celebration is in order," Pepper said. "I have yet to be told what it is."

"It's two in the morning."

"Goodness, already?" Katherine asked. "Hurry up with those glasses and drinks."

"Ryan Streeter is right. You are bossy." But Pepper did as Katherine said, emptying the last of the liquid into a third glass. "Okay. Now, what are we celebrating?"

Katherine arranged the drinks on an old tray. "I'll tell you outside. We've wasted enough of that moonlight."

Katherine led with the drinks. Lila followed close behind with as many white candles as she could carry. Pepper looked around the old-fashioned kitchen for something to bring, but they'd taken everything. She trounced out after them empty-handed. When Lila placed the candles on solid ground, Pepper snatched the matches. "I can help. I'm not totally incapable, you know."

Lila looked as surprised as Pepper was, but she handed the matches over.

The night was quiet. The air, although still heavy with humidity, was much cooler now. Lila was already swaying, her dance so Bohemian Pepper wondered about her ancestors. She was almost jealous. Years ago her grandfather had traced the Bartholomew family beyond the *Mayflower*. Every one of Pepper's genes was present and accounted for and practically stamped with nobility.

She wished there were a Gypsy thread somewhere. She would have settled for one scandalous love affair resulting in something wild and impetuous.

"Smell that arborvitae and freshly mowed grass," Lila called.

Pepper sniffed. "I smell sulfur." But she blew out the last match and she had to admit there was something pleasant in the air. The candlelight *was* beautiful, the moonlight even better. She sighed. "All that's missing is a man."

"We don't need a man," Lila insisted.

"Maybe you don't."

Lila did an interesting little move that reminded Pepper of Tinkerbell with two left feet. And Pepper knew her jealousy was misdirected.

"Pretend we're Amazon women," Lila called.

"*If* the Amazons ever existed, they became extinct, probably due to their aversion to M-E-N."

"I said pretend."

"Fine." Pepper assumed her favorite pose, a hand on one hip, most of her weight on her right foot. "It's not working."

She'd been feeling edgy for days. She didn't particularly like country life. It was too quiet, too dark, even with that moon. She would have enjoyed a diversion. "There's just nothing like a man in the middle of your bed." She found Katherine and Lila looking at her. "Don't mind me. I haven't had sex since I left Paris."

"It's been eight months for me," Lila said very quietly.

Suddenly, nobody was dancing.

"Is that what we're celebrating?" Pepper asked, eyeing Katherine shrewdly. "Did you get laid tonight?"

"For heaven's sake!" Lila said.

"I wish," Katherine said.

Moonbeams bleached the colors out of the night, turning the entire world white, black and silver, making it difficult to tell if Katherine was blushing. But there was trouble in paradise, and Pepper knew she wasn't jealous of Katherine Avery, either. She didn't know what was wrong with her.

"What are we celebrating, if not that?" Lila asked, linking arms with Pepper.

Finally, Katherine passed out the drinks. "Your online auction was supposed to end at twelve o'clock sharp, but there was so much activity I left it open an hour longer. It was like throwing gasoline on a fire."

"So what did Pearl Ann's instructions bring?"

Lila nudged her with one shoulder.

"Two thousand dollars!" Katherine declared.

"Two thousand dollars?" Lila repeated.

Katherine nodded.

"For *take things out with a broom handle, rinch and starch?*" Pepper asked.

"For that, *Myrtle Ann's* old washtub and her grandmother's diary," Katherine said.

"Two thousand dollars!" Pepper faced Lila. "We're rich!" she exclaimed, as if she didn't routinely spend that much in an afternoon on Rodeo Drive.

Lila tipped her face up, letting the moonlight wash over her. Since Pepper was the closest, she was the one who caught Lila's drink before it slipped through her fingers. Lila's arms were outstretched, her eyes closed, her hair hanging long and shimmery down her back. She was losing herself in this celebration, a gypsy around a fire.

Katherine had wandered away from any obstacles such as glasses and flames, and was doing the same, except her dance was more like a waltz. "Do you know what my mama would call this if she were here?"

"What?" So Lila *was* listening.

"Skylarking," Katherine said.

"Romping with words."

Katherine and Lila both glanced at Pepper.

"You seem surprised I knew that."

"Not surprised," Katherine said. "Pleased."

All the ire drained out of Pepper, every last ounce. She didn't have to prove herself to these women any more than she had to prove herself to her grandfather.

The revelation was startling in its simplicity and required more thought. But not here. Not now. Right now she was on a different track. "Do you know what I need?" she asked loud enough for both of them to hear.

"We already covered that," Lila answered.

Pepper wondered if she was the only one who heard the smile in Lila's voice, and she realized that Lila was happy here. "Besides that," Pepper insisted.

"What do you need?" Katherine asked.

"I need to prove myself to myself and I don't have a clue how to do that."

"Close your eyes," Katherine called.

"I was there when Lila fell for that, remember?"

"Then leave your eyes open," Lila said. She sounded giddy. Tipsy. And she hadn't even sampled her drink. She was getting drunk on moonbeams.

Pepper wondered if that was where the word moonshine originated. She loved words. She always had. It occurred to her that she and Katherine were a lot alike. Both were fluent in French and Francis Thompson. They were both well bred and bossy, and neither seemed to know where they were supposed to go from here.

Spreading her hands wider, Lila said, "All right, you two. I'm asking the universe for its help."

When Lila stopped dancing and opened her eyes, Pepper asked, "Are you getting anything?"

Lila shook her head. "But I have the strongest sensation that I'm exactly where I'm supposed to be. And knowing that is enough." She looked at Katherine. "What about you? What do you need?"

"I think I need the same thing Pepper needs."

"You need to prove something to yourself?"

"No. Your other need."

"You mean you and the mayor—"

"Haven't in a very long time." Katherine bent at the knees and swooped like a forest nymph. "But I'm working on it."

"Hell," Pepper said, "Let's all work on that one!"

Three shadows danced across the dewy grass. Without realizing it, one of them had supplied a reason to laugh, one a reason to dance and one a reason to believe.

The universe supplied the moonlight.

Joe was sitting on the stoop, waiting for the cabin to cool down when Lila, Pepper and Katherine drifted out of the big house. He was too far away to hear their conversation, but he could tell them apart all the way from here. One was tall and svelte, one was of average height and slightly hippy—it was all that real butter southern women used—and one was petite and winsome. If he wasn't mistaken, they were all in their pajamas. They appeared to be celebrating. He couldn't imagine what they had in common, let alone what they had to celebrate.

Apparently that didn't matter. They laughed and talked and danced. Every once in a while, they took a sip of something, and the laughing, dancing and talking commenced all over again.

He didn't understand Katherine's connection to Lila and Pepper, but he had to admit he hadn't heard her laugh this way in a very long time. She wasn't the only one laughing. Not even Ricky and Ryan had made this much racket yesterday when they'd decided to ride the goats. This wasn't the cackle of an old woman or the twitter of young boys. This laughter was clear and lyrical, and contagious enough to make even him smile.

The goats were awake. Instead of ramming something hard with their heads, they stood as still as the night, watching. Joe didn't believe for a minute they'd learned manners. There was something else at work here. And whatever it was, it was bringing The Meadows back to life.

It was bringing him back to life, too.

He wondered how long the party would go on. He would have liked to watch until the end. They wouldn't have known, any more than they knew that he got up and went inside. But he knew, and more and more, that was enough.

CHAPTER 9

The only thing keeping Katherine upright in her chair, daintily stirring cream into her coffee instead of slumped over her everyday breakfast china, was proper upbringing. She was actually entertaining the notion of going back to bed. Not that she would. She never went back to bed, not even when she had the flu, and she didn't have the flu. She wasn't sick. She was tired. That tended to happen to people who stayed out until four in the morning.

Goodness, she was smiling. She started guiltily, but unless Heath could see through the Political section of the newspaper, the only section that wouldn't keep until after supper, her *faux pas* remained her little secret.

When had smiling become a *faux pas*?

Bringing the coffee she'd been stirring back into focus, she took a sip. That took care of her smile, for there was nothing worse than the taste of lukewarm coffee. That was the price she paid for daydreaming.

She topped her cup off with piping hot coffee from the stainless steel carafe on the tray in the center of the table. Much better, she thought as she lowered the cup back to the saucer, as her mama had taught her. She wondered what her mama would say about her little celebration last night.

She wondered what Heath would say.

She had half a mind to reach across the table and rip the damn newspaper out of his hands and ask him. That might get a rise out of him. Was that what she wanted? She wasn't sure she was ready for that, although last night she'd almost gotten a rise out him, ready or not.

He'd been waiting up for her when she'd returned from The Meadows. She hadn't expected that.

He'd been worried about her, he'd said.

She'd left him a note, she'd said.

He'd read the note, he'd said.

He'd wanted to know where she'd been, but hadn't asked. The need to had been between them just as much as the question itself. Maybe he would have gotten around to asking, but she'd crawled into bed and promptly fell asleep.

Had she really gotten tipsy on moonlight and mint juleps? Her? Her mama used to say there was a wildfire inside Katherine just waiting for a spark to ignite it. Heath had been that spark. One kiss and she'd gone up like dry tinder.

They'd been in their third year at the University

of Virginia in Charlottesville when they met. He was a political science major and she was enrolled in the school of arts. He used to walk past her dance class Monday and Wednesday mornings. He'd been a creature of habit even then. Then, she'd been too in love to notice.

He'd once told her he noticed her legs first but fell in love with her mind. She still had good legs and a sharp mind. A lot of good either of those things did her.

And whose fault was that?

"Tired this morning?" he asked from behind his newspaper.

She stared at the back of his paper, trying to decide what to say. "It isn't what you're thinking, Heath."

Hadn't she said the same thing last week to Pepper and Lila? What was the old adage?

The more loudly one proclaims innocence, the more guilty the conscience.

She had no reason to feel guilty for having a little fun last night, and she didn't want him to get the wrong impression about it. "That online auction brought in more money than I'd expected. I drove out to The Meadows to tell Lila and Pepper. We wound up celebrating."

"How?" He looked at her over the top of his paper.

Eye contact first thing in the morning. Well, well. Taking another sip of coffee, she said, "We had mint juleps. Pepper made them."

"Did you tell her that most people in the south don't drink mint juleps and that it's just one of many stereotypical misconceptions?"

"I decided to let her discover that on her own. Besides, they were very good." She allowed herself to feel the warm glow from the poignant memory before adding, "And we danced."

"You danced?"

"Outside. In the moonlight. Just the three of us. And the goats."

He disappeared behind the paper. "I would have liked to have seen that."

Was he flirting with her?

Heat gathered at the base of her throat, spreading outward to her arms, her legs, her fingers and toes. Perhaps there was still one tiny ember left in her. And in him.

She finished her oatmeal and marmalade toast and he finished his corn flakes and fruit. She was so familiar with every sound, every rustle, every crunch. Even the clank of their dishes as they carried them to the kitchen was as natural as the sound of her own breathing. But something was different this morning. It was as if the atmosphere was charged with a new energy.

"Do you hear that?" she asked.

He listened. "All I hear is the rain."

She gaped at him.

"It started fifteen minutes ago. I assumed you'd noticed."

She ran to the window. The sky was a haze of gray. Water sluiced down the windowpanes and raced through downspouts, the branches on the maple tree sagging beneath the added weight.

"The farmers and orchard growers can relax," he said, straightening his tie and reaching for his umbrella. "The drought is over."

Not quite, she thought as she rinsed their dishes and loaded them into the dishwasher, but it was a start.

Lila was in the dining room when Pepper finally got up. "Now *that's* a rain cloud," she said, glancing up from the papers spread across the table.

"Very funny." Pepper stretched and yawned. "Did you know we were doing a rain dance last night?"

Lila rolled her eyes because they hadn't been doing any such thing. She didn't know what time the shower had started. It had been clear when she'd gone to bed at four, and raining when she woke up at ten. She'd scooted to the edge of the bed and looked out the window, which had been open when she'd gone to sleep. Pepper must have heard the rain, gotten up, closed all the windows and then gone back to bed.

Another side of Pepper was coming to light. The Bartholomews had built their fortune steadily from the railroads to their current status as the owners of one of the largest hotel chains in the world. They weren't quite the Hiltons, but they certainly rubbed shoulders with them. Pepper had had every imaginable opportunity, but she wasn't the spoiled little heiress people said she was. She could get her hands dirty if she had to. And she could see to a friend's needs, too.

Treading lightly so as not to wake her, Lila had thought about that, and about a dozen other things as she'd wandered through the house this morning, seeing it anew. All that remained of Myrtle Ann's clutter was a collection of fancy teacups and saucers, a tin of skeleton keys, a jar of buttons, a few fringed lamps and the antiques Lila had decided to use. Her furniture from Providence fit in comfortably here, and the modern touches such as the laptops, coffeemaker, cell phones, Gucci handbags and flip-flops she and Pepper had added brought the home into the current century.

Pepper sat down across from Lila at the table. "That was some party last night. You're looking very pleased about something this morning."

Lila shrugged. Earlier, she'd caught her reflection in the living room mirror, seeing herself anew, too. She wasn't slightly psychic anymore, at least not in the sense she'd once been. Even last night in the moonlight, she'd experienced no buzz, no whispers, no visions. And yet this morning she knew exactly why Myrtle Ann had left The Meadows to her. And knowing brought a sense of purpose to her life that had been missing for more than eight months now.

"What are you doing?" Pepper asked.

"I've been going over all the information I can find about Noreen McCaffrey's disappearance. You and Katherine have both said it. Myrtle Ann brought me here for a reason. I think she wanted me to help Joe find out what happened to Noreen. And I want you to help me."

"Me?"

Lila pushed some of the articles across the table. "Lately you've been showing your true colors. I've always known you were a wonderful friend, but you're more than a rich girl with great taste in clothes and anything French. You're smart, Pepper."

"Flattery will get you everywhere."

Lila took a moment to acknowledge the warm glow Pepper's cynicism brought to the friendship. "Then you'll help me help Joe find Noreen?"

Instead of answering, Pepper put her London Fog raincoat on over her pajamas and went outside. Lila grabbed the pink umbrella off the peg on her way by and went to stand beside Pepper at the porch railing. "What's bothering you?"

"Are you sure you want to find Noreen? I mean, I've seen the way you and Joe look at each other."

"It's possible I need my head examined."

"That's true. Don't look so stricken," Pepper said. "I get the distinct impression Joe feels the same way about you."

"That's supposed to make me feel better?"

"Noreen's been gone a long time. Besides, a lot of married people get carried away by an attraction to someone other than their spouses some time or other, don't they? You should know. You used to help couples repair relationships all the time."

Why on earth that put Lila in mind of Katherine, she didn't know. Pepper must have been thinking the same thing, because she said, "There's a connection between Joe and Katherine."

"What kind of connection?" Lila hated to say it out loud.

"What kind do you think?"

"She said it wasn't what we were thinking."

"What else could it be?" Pepper asked. "You're getting yourself in deep, and there's a good chance it won't have a happy ending."

"Spoken like a true pessimist."

Pepper blew out all her breath. She examined her fingernails and then shook her head. "Do you want to tell Joe or shall I?"

Lila smiled before giving Pepper a hug. "I knew I could count on you."

"Now I'm predictable, too? I am getting old."

Just then the goats came charging around the corner of the house. They splashed through puddles like their human namesakes.

"How did they get out?" Pepper asked.

"Maybe Joe let them out to milk them." All three animals raced past the barn without ramming their heads into anything, then disappeared over the hill toward Joe's cabin, energized by the rain. Humans and animals weren't so different.

The sound of the rain cascading over the roof reminded Lila of water spilling over a small waterfall. Last night when she'd danced in the dark, sound had carried for miles. Today the sky was made up of a dome of clouds that seemed to touch the ground all around, holding sounds close to the earth. "Now listen," she said.

Pepper slipped her hood off her head. "What am I listening to?"

"The earth breathing. Do you hear it?"

"I hear the garden growing. It sounds like money to me."

They were standing side-by-side on the grass now, and Lila held the umbrella over Pepper's head, too. "What are you going to spend your third of the money from that online auction on?"

"Food comes to mind. Something steamed, not fried. And something other than peanut butter. I think I'll reinvest part of the rest in our fruit and vegetable stand. Look. Here comes Joe. What's he doing?"

Lila squinted through the rain. Joe was running toward them up the lane, donning a shirt, yelling something.

"What's he saying?" Pepper asked.

He yelled again.

"What?" Pepper yelled back.

Lila turned her head and listened. "Did he say goats?"

"The goats!"

They were frolicking in the middle of the wild-flower garden closest to the road. Lila and Pepper ran across the driveway, waving their arms and yelling, "Shoo!"

The goats seemed to think it was great fun.

"We're making it worse!" Pepper cried.

Lila ran to the gate and opened it, then spoke to the goats in a low, stern tone of voice. The animals stopped, looked and listened. One by one, they returned to the corral.

"What are you?" Pepper asked Lila. "The goat whisperer? What did you say to them?"

Lila smiled a Cheshire cat smile.

Joe was breathing heavily when he finally reached them. The rain darkened his hair and ran into his eyes as he said, "She threatened to let Ryan and Ricky ride them every day if they didn't get out of her garden."

"*Our* garden," Lila said. "It's a group project. I take it Rusty isn't coming today?"

"There's not much for him to do in the rain."

He drew himself away from her the way he often did, but they both knew it was only a matter of time before he had to do it again. They were drawn to one another, like bees to honey, waves to the shore, two lonely souls who weren't as lonely now.

"And if Rusty doesn't come, Ryan and Ricky won't be here, either," Lila said. "And Katherine won't be bringing lunch."

"Dinner."

"I stand corrected." She smiled.

And he almost did.

Pepper held her hand in front of her face. Turning it over, she mumbled something in French before saying, "Lila's ready to make that trade, Joe."

Although he didn't say anything for what felt like a long time, Lila could tell he understood exactly what Pepper meant.

"I'll leave you two to work out the details," Pepper said. "I'll be inside, starting the coffee, since no one else seems to have done it."

Joe and Lila watched her traipse into the house, her slippers splashing in puddles as she went. "Last night," Joe said after she disappeared inside the house, "when you were dancing, I finally realized it was enough that I know I didn't hurt Noreen."

"You saw us dancing?"

"I caught the first act. Are you sure about what you're proposing, Lila?"

It was the first time he'd called her by name. She wished she didn't like it so much. "You would have better luck if you went to a bona fide psychic."

"I don't want a bona fide psychic."

It wasn't difficult to read between those lines. Rather than dwell on what he *did* want, she mulled over everything she'd read regarding the day Noreen went missing. There had to be something she'd overlooked, something everyone had overlooked. "I think it's time you told me about Noreen, don't you?"

He stared hard at her, the rain falling between them. "Can you be ready in an hour?" he asked.

"Ready for what?"

"I'll take you through the house where Noreen, Chloe and I used to live."

"And you'll tell me about them?" she asked.

"I'll tell you anything you want to know."

The McCaffrey house sat on a hill on the outer edge of Murray where the valley began its gradual rise toward the mountains. Lila had heard the house was magnificent. Magnificent didn't do it justice.

She shivered, which was strange since the sun had come out and turned the valley into a sauna. Nerves, she told herself. Of course she was nervous. There was a lot at stake here.

Joe wasn't expecting her to have a vision or a psychic experience. She was here as a friend who believed in his innocence. If she happened to sense something, great. If not, so be it. Remember that, she told herself.

He opened the gate with a remote control, and parked in the circle driveway in front of the house. Her first sensation upon entering the marbled foyer wasn't of Noreen McCaffrey, but of twenty-foot ceilings and artificially cooled air. Immediately, Lila's eyes were drawn to a large family portrait in the living room. It was the only adornment on the entire wall. That in itself said, *Look at me*.

"She's beautiful," Lila said, walking closer for a better look.

"Beauty can be deceiving."

Hearing her own thoughts echoed in his voice raised goose bumps on her arms again. Rubbing them, she said, "Your daughter has her coloring. How old was Chloe when this was taken?"

"She was eleven. Noreen hired the photographer just before she disappeared."

Lila wondered if that was relevant. Why would a woman have a family portrait taken if she was planning to disappear?

Concentrating on the photograph, she noted the diamonds in Noreen's ears and on her fingers. Her sweater had to be cashmere. It matched her brown eyes perfectly. Everything about her looked tasteful, except the cleavage on display.

Lila seemed to recall reading that Noreen had been born in Vegas and had grown up in L.A. Both places were a long way from Murray, Virginia.

"How did the two of you meet?"

"Do you want the truth?"

Lila hadn't realized he was so close behind her.

"Or do you want the version we told Chloe?"

"The truth. Always the truth." She hoped he did them both a favor and left out the details.

Moving to stare out the window, he said, "She was in my bed the morning after I pitched my first no-hitter in the majors. Chloe was born nine months later."

In the portrait, Chloe McCaffrey's blond hair nearly reached her waist. There were freckles across her nose, making Lila wonder if there was a tomboy lurking beneath that velvet and lace. Her hand was in her mother's, and Joe had an arm around both of them. They might have been an ordinary wealthy family, like Pepper's family. Except Noreen McCaffrey had disappeared, and nearly everyone believed Joe had had something to do with it. For all her training, Lila still didn't understand why it was so much easier for people to believe the worst in others. It wasn't one of humans' more attractive traits.

Joe gave her a tour of the rest of the downstairs. Most of the rooms were opulently furnished. The kitchen contained every imaginable gadget. She couldn't help looking at the knife set near the industrial cooktop.

The police had found traces of Noreen's blood on a doorknob, and Joe's fingerprints on several of the knives, which only proved what those people the police had interviewed had said. The McCaffreys had had guests over for dinner a few nights prior to Noreen's disappearance, and Joe had done the cooking.

"Who did you have over that night?" Lila asked.

"Two of the guys from the team and their wives were in town, so I invited them to stay and eat. Noreen pouted most of the evening because Pete Norris and Phil Bailey and I talked baseball."

"And you and Noreen argued after everyone left?"

"She thought Phil's wife was coming on to me."

"Was she?" Lila asked.

They'd reached the den, which housed a large-screen television and was decorated in a baseball theme. "Not that I noticed. Noreen always thought someone was coming on to me."

"That suggests insecurity," she said.

"It got old." He slid a hand into the pocket of his navy chinos and jiggled his keys.

"Is it true that you told her you wished she was dead?"

His throat convulsed, but he nodded. "In a public restaurant, loud enough for several people to overhear."

The circumstantial evidence was very damning.

"I wish I hadn't said it, not because I didn't feel that way at the time, but because little girls should never have to read something like that in the papers."

"Tell me about Chloe."

Joe's entire demeanor changed, and he relaxed. "No matter what Noreen claimed, I've never been sorry we had her. I was pitching a double-header in Texas when Noreen went into labor. I took the call from the dugout. Don Ackerman threatened to bench me for the rest of the season if I didn't finish out that game."

"And did you finish?"

He shook his head.

"Did he bench you?"

Again, he shook his head.

"Did he often make empty threats?" she asked, wishing he would be a little more forthcoming with the details regarding his life with Noreen. This way felt like pulling teeth.

"Coaches want to win."

"Did you make it home in time?"

"I got there just as she was being born." He smiled for the first time. "My little girl came into the world mad and she wasn't afraid to let everyone know it. She hasn't been the same the last few years."

Everything came back to Noreen's disappearance. Lila understood the workings of the human mind well enough to know that failing to deal with an issue never made it go away. In fact, avoidance made it the number one priority because the mind focused all its energy on whatever was being avoided. It required great concentration to pretend something didn't exist. The mind was never fooled.

Noreen's disappearance couldn't be more glaring if it were on a marquee in flashing lights. What really happened to Noreen McCaffrey? Did she leave of her own accord? Had someone else harmed her? If so, who?

She thought about those questions as she followed Joe upstairs. There, she had a hazy impression of more large rooms and opulent furnishings.

He walked as far as the door of the master bedroom but didn't go in. Pointing to a closed door, he said, "I slept down the hall. There's something I haven't told anyone else."

Lila turned slowly. "I'm listening."

"I wanted a divorce."

"Did Noreen know?"

"I told her the week before she disappeared."

"How did she take it?" Lila asked.

"Better than I'd expected." A muscle worked in Joe's jaw. "I figured she'd take me to the cleaners, but by then, I didn't care. I just wanted out."

"Why didn't you tell the police?"

"I didn't feel like handing them another nail for my coffin."

Lila could feel her heart beating and tried to calm herself by focusing on Chloe's room. The walls were hand-painted murals of fairies and butterflies and everything little girls loved, the bed a canopy Lila used to dream about when she was a child. "This room is fit for a princess. I don't understand why Noreen would have had a room decorated like this and then send Chloe to boarding school to live."

"I was gone eight months of the year. Noreen tired of being solely responsible for her."

"What did she do while you were gone?"

"Whatever she wanted."

"Did she and Chloe visit you on the road?"

Joe passed a tapestry wall hanging in the hall. "When Chloe was little, they came every month. It was such fun." He paused, as if reliving poignant memories. "Noreen could be charming and vibrant and alluring. I saw less and less of that side of her as the years went by. After she sent Chloe to boarding school, they stopped visiting me on the road altogether."

They ended the tour back in the living room, and Lila found herself staring up at the portrait once again. *Where are you?* she asked Noreen's image.

If ever she needed her sixth sense, it was now. But the only sensation she felt was in the pit of her stomach, never a good sign.

Joe watched Lila from a distance. He'd noticed she often wore dresses, not the loose-fitting kind that hung like old-fashioned flour sacks, but sleeveless dresses that skimmed her hips and hinted at curves without revealing them. She was staring up at the portrait so intently he wondered what she saw. In the picture, Noreen's diamond ring glared from her finger. He'd bought it for her a year before the photo was taken, after one of her uglier fits of jealousy. It had kept her happy for a few months. Nothing ever kept Noreen happy for long. Not even their daughter. He searched Chloe's expression in the photograph, looking for the old glint. But it wasn't there, at least not in that pose.

"Chloe wouldn't smile for the photographer that day," he said. "No matter what he tried."

"Why wouldn't she?" Lila asked, looking at Chloe's image now.

"She'd just gotten braces, and she hated them."

Joe fished his wallet out of his back pocket. He

opened it, removed a small photo and showed it to Lila. He watched her take a closer look.

"I thought he couldn't get her to smile."

"He couldn't, so I leaned down and whispered in her ear. She burst out laughing, and the photographer snapped this picture."

Lila studied the smaller image. Noreen looked as if she'd just gotten a whiff of something offensive, and Joe wasn't even looking at the camera. But Chloe was, and she looked happy enough for all of them.

"I can see why you carry this one in your wallet. What did you say to make her laugh?"

He took the photo back and looked at it again before returning it to his wallet. "I told her all that metal was sure to help our television reception. The kid used to have a wacky sense of humor."

"Like her father?" Lila asked.

"More like her grandfather. Although Dad hasn't laughed much lately, either."

There it was again, the monkey on all their backs. "What time are you leaving for Philadelphia?" Lila asked.

"First thing in the morning."

That ended the tour. Lila waited on the front steps while he turned out the lights and locked the door. They were both quiet until they were heading across town.

"Now that you've seen the house, what do you think?" he asked.

"I don't think I'm going to like Noreen." She hadn't meant to say that.

"That suggests you feel she's alive."

She glanced out the window. "It does, doesn't it?"

"What's the standard operating procedure in these situations?" he asked.

"Standard operating procedure?"

"What do you typically do after you attempt to tap into your intuition?"

"When I was a child, my mother always prepared me a huge meal. She still believes the answer to every ailment is food. Feed a fever. Feed a cold. Feed a feeling. It's a wonder I don't weigh three hundred pounds. We'd eat, we'd dance in the moonlight if it wasn't cloudy, and she'd tuck me into bed."

If she were to wet her lips, she knew she would taste her shoe. Talk about putting her foot in it.

"Would you settle for a burger back at my place?" He was looking straight ahead. He wasn't smiling, but the line beside his mouth deepened from the effort not to.

"Joe?" she said, warming to his style, among other things. "I wouldn't consider it settling."

He made a U-turn at the Welcome to Murray sign. And Lila made a mental note to pick up her stomach the next time she passed by this way.

CHAPTER 10

Lila stood perfectly still, her sandals dangling from one finger, heat rising in waves off the wooden dock beneath her feet. Dragonflies skimmed the surface of the pond, their wings iridescent in the sun. Joe had started the grill, and smoke rose straight into the air. Neither of them had mentioned Noreen since leaving his house in town, but Lila was growing more and more convinced the woman was alive. *Then where is she?* The question burned the back of her mind as she tested the water with her big toe.

"It's spring-fed," Joe called, arranging the burgers on the grill. "That's the reason it's so clear and cool."

"In a thousand years geologists will probably go to a lot of trouble to find a scientific reason there are so many flat stones on the bottom."

"Think they'll figure it out?" he asked, skipping one across the water.

Joining Joe on shore, she picked up a stone and tried her hand at it. Hers sank with a single gu-loop.

"You make it look so easy," she said. "You're a natural-born pitcher. Do you miss it?"

"I was getting too old, anyway."

"Before Noreen disappeared, you'd pitched back-to-back record-breaking seasons. You were at your peak and you know it."

"Are you trying to make me feel better or worse?"

"Sorry," she said, drowning a second stone. "I used to be eloquent and witty."

"Do you miss it?"

His dry wit surprised her, but the subtle shifting of his expression made her glad she'd taken a little time with her appearance this afternoon. They seemed to have developed a pattern of advance and retreat. She couldn't help wondering how it was going to turn out.

Wading to her ankles, she looked all around. The path disappeared into the orchard to the north. A hazy mist shrouded the foot of the mountains to the east, and to the south, pastureland descended to a deep ravine. From here, all that was visible to the west was the big house and outbuildings.

"We're secluded here, aren't we?" She averted her face, wondering why she didn't simply tell him she was hot for his body.

"Your own private piece of paradise." He dropped the remaining stones. "Do you like ponds and lakes?

Or do you prefer the ocean and waves breaking and white beaches?"

"I like swimming pools. And I like the sky. Did you know that's where I saw Holly Baxter? Her face appeared in the clouds last October."

"Whatever happened to the Jezebel, anyway?"

Wading in a little deeper, she said, "Her daddy whisked her off to Europe 'to study.'" She made quote marks with her fingers.

"And lover boy?"

"The last I knew Alex was working in wills and trusts, the bane of an attorney's existence. He had a brilliant future."

"Are you over him?"

"May he grow old in some windowless basement office."

Joe said, "Thank goodness there are no hard feelings."

"Forgive and forget is my motto."

"Right. Mine, too." Joe removed his shoes and socks and rolled up the cuffs of his pants. Wading into the water, he said, "Sex gets a lot of people in trouble. Some say it's at the root of all evil."

He'd left her the perfect opportunity to say, "Is there something going on between you and Katherine, Joe?"

"Katherine? And me? You mean an affair? No.

Hell, no. I haven't been unfaithful to Noreen. I'm pretty sure that's about to change."

She spun around as he took a step toward her. "Do you think that's wise?"

"It would be wise if I moved back to my house in town." He took another step toward her. "Or somewhere else, anywhere else that isn't here, near you."

"But you're not going to?" she asked.

"I will if you ask me to."

That was exactly what she should do. Instead, she took a step toward him. Unfortunately, she tripped over a rock she'd avoided a minute ago, and landed with a splash in a foot of water.

"You okay?"

Her pride and her rear end stung a little, but she wasn't about to admit that. "Do you know what I always dreamed of being when I was a little girl?"

Holding out his hand to help her up, he said, "A ballerina?"

She tugged hard on his outstretched hand for that last crack. The momentum caught him off balance and he tumbled over, too. She scooted out of the way and jumped to her feet, but the water slowed her down. He lunged, snagging her ankle, and she toppled over again. Their shouts and laughter rang out as they rolled in the cool water, splashing and playing like she hadn't played in years.

She wound up on his lap, facing him, straddling him, her dress floating around her hips. His eyes were steady, his breathing deep, his hands on either side of her waist, drawing her even closer. She didn't need any help finding his mouth with hers.

It was the kind of kiss women dream of, the kind of kiss that was a prelude to more, the kind of kiss that made a woman feel completely understood.

A chain reaction started where their mouths were joined, warmth rippling like heat waves, stoking her desire. For months she'd felt so disconnected to her former self, and suddenly his kiss grounded her, possessive and hungry, an urgent mating of instinct and emotion. She liked this man, and what he was doing with his lips and tongue and his hands. Need uncurled in places physically unconnected, reminding her that everything and everyone was somehow connected. How could she have forgotten the most fundamental law of the universe?

She drew away slowly when it was over, and dazedly got to her knees. He found his feet in a similar fashion, then helped her the rest of the way up. Neither of them spoke of the kiss, but it remained between them like a promise as they went hand-in-hand to the grassy shore.

The burgers were smoking as they reached the shore. He took them off the grill before going inside for condiments, sodas and towels. When he returned, they carried their plates to the rowboat and sat on the wooden seats to eat.

Her hair dried in tangles; his stuck straight up in front. If anyone had come along, they would have assumed they'd spent the afternoon in bed. As far as Joe was concerned, it wouldn't have mattered if someone had seen them. He didn't care what people thought anymore. He'd picked a hell of a time to make that discovery, for Lila had just agreed to help him find Noreen.

"There's still time to reconsider, Joe."

He wondered if she realized how often she seemed to read his mind. "I won't reconsider," he said. "I've had a good time this afternoon."

"You enjoyed going through your house in town?"

"I enjoyed after more." He told himself not to expect a reply, then barely breathed while he waited for one.

"I've had a good time, too."

He found himself looking at her mouth. It was safer than looking lower. He intended to take this slow, to give her time to tell him no. She didn't, though. Instead, she began to tell him about her former patients and her clinic and her colleagues. She talked and talked. At one point, she said, "I don't know what's wrong with me. Normally, I listen."

"Today," he said, "let me do the listening."

It was as if a levee had failed and her words spilled over the break. Once she started, she couldn't seem to stop. She continued while he took her up to the barn and showed her where he kept the feed for the goats and chickens. As he showed her how to change the animals' water, she told him about her fear of the ocean and her love of night. While he demonstrated the proper way to milk the goats, a chore she would have to do while he was away, she told him about her father, who'd made getting married an art form and was currently living in the Australian outback with wife number five. She seemed surprised when she began to tell him about her public humiliation, but that came spilling out, too.

She was telling him about the day Pepper had appeared out of the blue just as Lila was leaving Providence, when he jotted down Rusty Streeter's phone number on the back of a gas receipt and slipped it into her hand. Folding her fingers over it, he held her hand for a moment in both of his. The simple gesture started a chain of complicated reactions. Her voice trailed away, her eyes on his.

"I didn't mean to make you stop," he said.

"You didn't. I was finished." Lila blinked, for it was true. She had no more words. She felt drained, purged. For months it was as if a fist had been wrapped around her vocal cords. The fist was gone. In its place she felt a burning inside, a yearning to strip off her wrinkled dress and press herself against him. Luckily, she didn't utter it aloud. Perhaps she was cured of saying what she was thinking precisely when she was thinking it.

They talked a little about the weather, and other nonpersonal subjects. Eventually, they parted ways. She hadn't gone far when he called her name.

"What did you dream of being when you were a kid? Besides a ballerina, I mean."

She considered fibbing, but wound up saying, "A concert pianist."

"Why aren't you?" he asked.

"Because I have two left thumbs to go with my two left feet."

His smile went straight to her head. "What about you?" she asked. "Did you ever dream of anything besides playing baseball?"

He shook his head.

And she said, "Sometimes new dreams come along when you least expect it."

"My thoughts exactly."

She wondered what he would do if she told him she already knew that. But was it psychic awareness? Or awareness of a more earthy, elemental kind?

He headed back to the cabin to get ready for his shift at McCaffrey's, and she followed the lane home.

Nothing had been settled, but one thing was certain. She wouldn't be asking Joe to leave The Meadows anytime soon.

On Friday morning Lila was concentrating so hard she didn't hear Pepper approach until she'd walked up behind her and said, "Well?"

And then it was too late. Lila jumped, causing the goat she was attempting to milk to jump, too, which resulted in a tipped-over milk bucket. "Pepper! You scared me."

"I can see that."

Lila righted the bucket, repositioned the stool, and tried again. The goat looked at her accusingly. "Don't worry," she said gently. "Joe will be back tomorrow evening." To Pepper, she said, "Do you want to give it a try?"

"That's just a little more intimate than I care to be with a goat. How did the tour go yesterday?"

Glad her face was averted, Lila said, "It went well, all things considered. I would have told you about it last night if you'd been here. Where were you?"

Pepper eased the rest of the way into the barn where Lila could see her without straining her neck. Wrinkling her nose at the offensive smell, Pepper said, "I paid a little visit to the horse track over in Charles Town."

"You went gambling?" Lila stopped attempting to

milk the poor goat and slowly stood up. She looked Pepper over judiciously, wondering what she was up to.

"How long have you been at this?" Pepper asked, pointing to the goat and the milking stool.

"An hour. Joe said it shouldn't take more than twenty minutes."

"Do you want me to call Rusty?"

"He's on his way over."

The friends looked closely at each other. Pepper hadn't been home when Lila finally fell asleep at midnight. It wasn't uncommon for her to fail to leave a note. Utterly independent, she'd once flown to Rome for a long weekend without telling a soul.

"You're up early." Lila eyed her friend. "You've already showered." Despite the drawstring, Pepper's coral skirt rode low on her hips, baring a narrow patch of skin at her waistline. "You're looking very put-together this morning. What did you really do last night?"

"What would you say if I told you I tripled my money?"

"You're telling me you bet your portion of the money from Katherine's online auction on a horse?"

Pepper handed over three hundred-dollar bills.

Staring at the crisp bills, Lila said, "Where did you really get this?"

"You don't believe I went to the horse races?"

"No, I don't."

Pepper's smile broadened in approval. "You've always had great instincts."

"You were testing me!" Lila threw up her hands. Darn this burgeoning admiration. "So where were you last night?"

"I went to a summer festival in Staunton."

"Then where did you get the money? Or do I want to know?"

"Katherine stopped by while you were out with Joe. She sold your Dutch armoire. The rest of your money is inside. Now stop stalling and tell me everything you learned during your tour of Joe's house. But let's move this inside. It smells horrid out here."

Rusty was pulling in as Lila and Pepper were leaving the barn. The first thing Pepper did upon entering the house was switch on the oscillating fan. She stood in front of it, listening intently as Lila relayed her impression of Joe's life with Noreen McCaffrey.

"Okay," she said, far more shrewd than most people gave her credit for. "What haven't you told me?"

Lila continued to organize the papers on the table as she decided how much more to say. "For starters, Noreen believed Joe was having an affair."

"With Katherine?" Pepper asked.

"Not her. With the wife of one of his teammates. I asked about Katherine, though. He said he never had an affair with anyone. He also said Noreen was extremely jealous. I got the impression she was a groupie who crawled into his bed with one intention. She got pregnant and he married her."

"Professional athletes are vulnerable to ambitious women. How will you feel if Noreen returns?"

Lila glanced toward the window, watching the play of light on the glass she'd washed earlier, on the pond in the distance, and on the clouds in the eastern sky. "Isn't that our goal?"

"Do you think she left of her own free will?"

Turning her back on the scenery outside the window, Lila said, "I think that's a very real possibility nobody seems to have pursued. As long as we're on the subject, there's something else you should know."

"You're making me nervous."

"You have to promise you won't breathe a word of this to another living soul, Pepper."

"I hate it when you do this." With a loud huff, she said, "Fine. I promise."

"A week before their last public argument, Joe told Noreen he wanted a divorce."

"Do the police know?"

"No."

"Why not?" Pepper asked.

"Because telling them would have given them another reason to believe he had a motive to kill her."

"Ya think?" Pepper quipped. "Noreen could have taken half of everything he'd worked so hard for. Men have killed for a lot less."

"What if she found a better way to ruin him? Something's been bothering me." Lila lifted the hair away from her damp neck and said, "Women who are as insecure as Noreen McCaffrey don't leave their husbands without having somebody else lined up."

"Do you think *she* was having an affair?" The fan fluttered the fabric of Pepper's short linen skirt. "Is anyone else in town missing?"

"I don't know," Lila said, "but I read that there is no such thing as a kept secret. Eventually, someone gets drunk or develops a conscience and the truth comes out. There are two places in every city or town where people go to bare their souls."

Pepper nodded. "One reason my hairstylist charges so much is because he's part creative genius, part shrink. What's the other place?"

"The local bars. We'll have to split up. People are guarded in groups, and we'll have a much better chance if we approach them one-on-one." She folded her arms at her ribs, strumming her fingers as she stared at Pepper. "So one of us is going to get her hair cut and one is going to get a little drunk. Do you have a preference?"

"I'm not ready to let anybody other than Dane have his way with my hair. I'll start with Joe's competition."

"You'll be careful?"

"I'll be careful," Pepper said. "Don't worry about your hair. It'll grow back."

The sign in the window of Darci's Curl Up And Dye said Walk-Ins Welcome. That alone made Pepper glad she wasn't the one going in, for she didn't trust a hairstylist who had room in his or her schedule. But Lila was on a mission, so after wishing her luck, Pepper drove over to Rebellion Street where the two main bars in Murray were located.

The General Lee sat on the third block. It had brick walls and scuffed hardwood floors and an antique bar Katherine Avery would have drooled over.

"What can I get you, Pepper, isn't it?" the bartender asked.

She ordered a cranberry juice and vodka, which seemed to meet with everyone's approval. Of course it did. She knew what she was doing.

The early-bird crowd was a mix of men and women, blue collar and professionals, old and young. Like the bartender, they all seemed to know who she was. The man sitting next to her introduced himself as Sawyer, just Sawyer. Although just-Sawyer had a deep indentation on his bare ring finger, she let him cozy up to her a little, even though she already knew how far it would—or in this case, wouldn't—go.

"What's a rich girl like you doing in a place like this?"

She couldn't even give him points for originality. "I'm waiting for my friend. She's around the corner getting her hair trimmed." She took a sip of her drink while he gave her one of those up, down, up again looks the opposite sex was notorious for. "As long as I'm here," she said, practically batting her eyelashes, "I'd like to conduct a survey."

She turned in her bar stool and spoke to Sawyer as well as the group of men closest to her. "How would you fill in these blanks? I like my women *blank*, my car *blank* and my shoes *blank*."

Sawyer went first. "Let's see. Women, cars and shoes, hmm? I like my women sexy, my car restored, and who the hell cares about shoes?"

She cast him a smile that told him he was clever. *Oh, brother.*

The bartender said, "I like my women stacked, cars are for sissies. I drive a truck, and I like my shoes comfortable."

Someone at a nearby table said he liked his women wild and his car revved. His buddy said he had it backwards. The shoe reference was dropped completely. Pepper didn't care. She was just priming them for the deeper questions.

She sipped her drink and laughed at jokes, some of which actually were funny. If they knew what she was doing, they didn't seem to mind. They didn't seem to mind talking about Joe, either, as long as she kept the topic about baseball. Eventually somebody brought up Noreen's name.

"Do you think she's alive?"

Pretty much everyone shrugged. It was as if they didn't care one way or the other. Interesting. Most people felt a crime was a crime and deserved punishment. Perhaps the fine folks of Murray believed Joe had done it; perhaps not. Pepper couldn't tell which way they leaned.

Sawyer fed some coins into the jukebox. Somebody else asked her to dance. She went a round or two when she noticed the group of professional-looking men stand up. She stopped dancing altogether as a man in a charcoal suit and sky-blue tie turned around. Heath Avery said hello on his way to the door. Everyone at the table except a tall accountant named Steve left with the mayor.

Letting the accountant buy her a drink, she said, "Is your meeting adjourned?"

"Nothing that formal," Steve said, pushing his glasses a little higher on his nose. "We were just discussing how to best present the new mileage proposal."

"I heard Heath Avery and Joe McCaffrey used to be good friends."

"I heard that, too."

After a few more of her questions were answered in a similar fashion, it became apparent that the only other useful information she was going to get out of Steve had to do with her retirement portfolio. She was about to move on to Joe's bar when a twentysomething guy named Doogie invited her to play a game of pool. She lined up her shot for the break and lucked out when two balls fell in. "Does Joe ever play pool with you guys?"

"He used to from time to time."

"What about his wife?" She lobbed the three into the corner pocket.

"What about her?" Doogie asked.

A waitress named Prudie brought another round of drinks while Pepper was lining up her next shot. Something about the way the woman looked at Pepper caused her to take a closer look as well.

"Did Noreen come here with him?" Pepper asked.

"She preferred the country clubs and spa resorts around D.C."

"She didn't have friends here?" Pepper asked, easing around to the other side of the billiards table.

"I suppose she had friends. Somewhere."

Talk about being evasive.

Pepper missed her shot, not purposefully; she was too competitive for that. After that Doogie ran the table.

Conceding defeat, Pepper was on her way to the door when Prudie caught up with her. "Noreen

McCaffrey was a user. She went through just about everybody in Murray. The Averys put up with her the longest, but eventually not even Katherine could stomach her."

"Do you know Heath and Katherine well?"

"I went to school with Heath. Everyone took to Katherine when he brought her home to Murray. She's class all the way, and not the goodie-goodie two-shoes kind, either. She used to volunteer at my Katie's school. She's a natural with little girls. Come back again, but next time, leave any mention of Noreen and Joe McCaffrey at the door, ya hear?"

The next thing Pepper knew she was staring at the lettering on the sign outside, wilting in the heat rising off the sidewalk and squinting against the blinding sun. Wondering if Lila was having better luck than she was, Pepper wasted no time seeking relief from the heat inside McCaffrey's Tavern a block away.

Although McCaffrey's had fewer drinkers at the bar than its competition, it didn't look much different to Pepper. The bartender bore a striking resemblance to Joe, though. Joseph McCaffrey Senior was busy drying glasses, and didn't look up, not even when she wiggled up onto her seat.

"I'd like some seltzer water with a wedge of lime, please."

He fumbled beneath the bar then slid a glass of clear liquid—with no lime—across the counter to her.

"You're Joe's father, aren't you?"

"No sense beating around the bush. You knew who I was before you came in."

"How nice that you're fluent in idioms."

"Did she just call you an idiot, Pop?" somebody behind her yelled.

"Don't blow your top, Sid," Joe Sr. said. "She's just chewing the fat while she waits for her girlfriend to get her ears lowered."

Sitting up a little straighter, Pepper knew when she'd been bested. She hadn't expected him to know what an idiom was. She most certainly hadn't expected him to pop three of the little acorns right back to her. She took a closer look. "How did you know Lila was getting her hair cut?"

Another man moseyed up to the bar before saying, "Not much gets past Pop, ain't that right, Pop?"

"*Isn't* that right," Pepper said before she could stop herself. "Don't mind me," she added apologetically. "My relatives are sticklers for proper English. I've been known to correct grammar on bathroom walls, but only if I've been drinking."

She knew she was forgiven when the man asked if he could buy her a drink. Doing her best to ignore the nicotine stains on his teeth, she said, "Thanks. I'd like that."

Joe Sr. set a draft beer down hard in front of her. For a split second, their eyes met. Pepper had never professed to have Lila's old talent, but she swore something invisible smacked her in the chin.

"I heard you were conducting a little survey down the street," Nicotine Harry said.

Pepper took a quick tally of McCaffrey's clientele. Sure enough, two of the men who'd been drinking with Doogie at The General Lee were here now. The end of the bar where that obnoxious man had been sitting the last time she was here was empty, but most of the tables were occupied. The jukebox was silent and nobody was playing pool. Everyone was too busy watching her to do anything else. Somehow Pepper didn't think the survey would go over as well with this crowd, so instead, she asked, "Do any of Joe Junior's old teammates ever stop by?"

There were a series of shrugs, a few head scratches, but the general consensus was no. She swore they took turns glancing covertly at Joe's dad.

"What about his old high school friends?" she asked.

"What are we?" somebody yelled. "Chopped liver?"

"Don't mind Grady," Nicotine Harry said. "He's three sheets to the wind."

"Close but no cigar," Grady yelled back, smarter than he looked.

"Noreen might have been a looker," someone else insisted, "but she couldn't hold a candle to you."

"Now you're blowing smoke," she said, raising her right eyebrow independently of her left. "This seems like a nice place. Tell me, do the city council members ever conduct their meetings here?"

Nobody answered, not even with an overused idiom.

"What about Noreen?" Pepper asked. "Did she ever venture into McCaffrey's?"

"She acted like she owned the place," Joe Sr. said. "Wait. In a sense, she did."

Pepper studied Joe Sr. for a long time, swirling the beer in her glass. He didn't look old enough to be Joe's father. He was on the tall side, had an average build and most of his hair. He had good teeth, although he bared them to snarl, not smile.

"How would you complete the following statement? she asked. "I like my women *blank*, my car *blank*, and my shoes *blank*."

The entire place got quiet. Apparently no one was going to say a word. Telling herself she should have listened to her first instinct and left well enough alone, she slid off the bar stool. She was halfway to the door when she heard Joe Sr. say, "I like my women intelligent, my car dependable, and my shoes under my own damn bed."

She was a block away before she realized he'd been trying to tell her something. Now who was behind the eight-ball? she wondered. She took a deep breath of hot, humid air and grimaced because she was thinking in idioms now.

The storekeepers up and down Rebellion Street were closing their doors. Other than a few women talking outside the diner and two old men shooting the breeze—Pepper cringed again—on a bench outside the barbershop, the only person on the sidewalk was the woman hurrying toward her.

She looked familiar. Very familiar.

"Lila?" Pepper came to a sliding halt. "Is that you?"

CHAPTER 11

"What's going on?" Chloe asked the instant Joe put the truck in park. "What are you doing? Why are you stopping?"

"The goats are out."

"I can see that. What are all these people doing here? Who's that woman in the funny-looking hat?"

He recognized Pepper, Katherine, Rusty, Ryan and Ricky. By process of elimination, he assumed the other woman was Lila, although it wasn't easy to tell in that hat. "That's Lila Delaney, the new owner of The Meadows I told you about."

The sound Chloe made through her nose was new this summer. He'd heard it often during the two-hundred-fifty-mile drive from Philadelphia to the Shenandoah Valley. In fact, his daughter had responded to his every attempt at conversation with a clipped "yes," "no," or her apparent all-time favorite, her new little snort.

"It's been a long drive and I'd like to freshen up."

He wondered when she'd developed this

penchant for making an innocent statement sound like an order. He was torn, and he wasn't proud of what that said about his uncertainty where parenting his daughter was concerned. Reaching a decision, he opened his door and got out. "This will only take a minute."

Katherine, Lila and Pepper waved their arms, sending the largest goat trotting away from them, straight toward the boys. One by one, Rusty, Ryan and Ricky lunged for him.

"You okay?" Joe asked the boy who ended up on the ground closest to him.

Ricky Streeter's face was red from exertion, his knees caked with mud. "The goats ate a whole row of Pepper's tomater plants. Now that they've had a taste, they won't even listen to Miz Delaney whisper to 'em."

Joe removed his belt.

"You gonna whup 'em?"

Joe wanted to wrap his arms around the boy and carry him off to a place where no one was ever whipped, not even goats. "And hurt them? No. If I have to, I'll use my belt for a leash. If we can get Buck tethered, I'm pretty sure the girls will be reasonable enough to follow."

Joe, Lila, Pepper, Katherine and the boys formed a half circle around the perimeter of the side garden where Buck was trampling the cucumber shoots and what was left of a row of tomato plants. The female goats watched with a great deal of interest as the humans slowly closed ranks, arms outstretched, driving Buck toward the corral.

"Chloe, ease around and open the gate, would you?" Joe called.

He was relieved when she did as he requested. Buck tried to make a run for it a few times, but after his attempts were thwarted, he trotted into the corral as if it had been his idea. Lila talked Nanny, Mo and Curly into joining him.

"Thank goodness you two came along when you did," Katherine said. "Hello, Chloe. Welcome to The Meadows. Have you met the Streeter brothers?"

"Didn't you use to go to our school?" eleven-year-old Ryan asked.

"Believe me, I've never gone to your school."

Ryan looked away, embarrassed. Joe wondered when his daughter had become a snob. He was still trying to decide how to best handle the situation when Katherine lured the boys to the house with mention of homemade macadamia nut cookies.

Chloe turned to Lila. "Dad said you're the new owner of this place."

Looking comical in a big, floppy denim hat, Lila said, "Myrtle Ann was generous enough to leave The Meadows to me. Pepper has been helping me and your father clear out the house and clean up the pastures and plant the vegetable and wildflower gardens."

Chloe glanced at Pepper. "Oh. Then you're the help."

Pepper's mouth dropped open.

"Chloe," Joe said, "that's not—"

Just then a gust of wind whisked Lila's hat off her head. Joe stared, speechless. Unfortunately, being struck speechless wasn't a family trait.

"No wonder you wear a hat," Chloe said, matter-of-fact.

"You know, kid—" Pepper began.

Lila stopped her with a firm shake of her head. "Pepper, why don't you go try Katherine's cookies. Save one for me, okay?"

Now that Joe had recovered from his initial shock, he said, "Have you done something different with your hair?"

"Are you referring to these stripes? I call the new color scheme neon carrot and everyday brown. Darci was trying to bring out the golden highlights. She assures me the orange will wash out after twenty-four shampoos."

"I'd be washing it every five minutes if I were you."

"Chloe!" Joe said, louder this time.

"I only had it done yesterday," Lila said. "You should have seen how bright it was ten shampoos ago. Would you care for one of Katherine's homemade cookies, Chloe?"

"No, thank you."

Joe said, "I told Chloe that you and Pepper are trying to help us find her mother."

"What can *you* do?" his daughter asked more sharply than Joe had expected.

"I used to be slightly psychic," Lila said.

Silence.

"She's not anymore," Joe said quietly.

"Obviously." Chloe looked straight at Lila's striped hair.

"Chloe, that's enough!" Joe said. "You've been home ten minutes and you already owe five people an apology."

She looked as if she'd been struck. Her lip quivered and her eyes were watery as she whispered, "This isn't my home." She spun around so fast her hair fanned out behind her. Her strut was a little wobblier than Pepper's had been, but no less regal.

After retrieving her denim hat, Lila said, "Pepper and I did some investigating while you were gone. If you have time after Chloe's settled, stop back and we'll tell you about it."

"Katherine's bossiness is rubbing off on you."

"I'll take that as a compliment. Welcome home, Joe."

The smile in Lila's voice matched the one on her

face. There was something warm and womanly in the way she was looking at him, and something purely enjoyable about the way he was responding.

He'd received standing ovations and cheers loud enough to make his ears ring, yet he'd never felt so much welcome in a woman's eyes. For the first time in a long time, it felt good to be home.

"This isn't easy to say," Lila whispered, holding on to the side of the rowboat.

Joe pulled hard on the oars, sending the boat and its midnight riders gliding smoothly and quietly across the water. When it had become apparent that Joe wasn't going to come back to the house tonight, Lila and Pepper had decided to stroll down to the cabin with a plate of Katherine's cookies. Joe had suggested taking the rowboat for a ride. He'd invited Chloe to come, too, but she'd professed to be too tired and had disappeared into the back bedroom.

"Just tell him," Pepper said, swatting another mosquito. "But hand me the repellant first, would you?"

Lila shot her a beseeching look.

"Don't look at me," Pepper said. "I'm only here as the chaperone, remember? By the way, Chloe just peeked out the window again. For a kid who refused to come along, she's awfully curious."

Resting the oars on the edge of the boat, Joe said,

"Whatever you've discovered couldn't be worse than what the police, media and my former fans have said about me."

Lulled by the gliding motion below and the stars and moon above, Lila whispered, "As far as you know, did Noreen ever have an affair?"

If the deep breath he took was an accurate indication, he didn't want to talk about this. "There were rumors."

Lilia understood that this was a difficult topic for Joe. Still, it would have been nice if he would elaborate a little. Since he didn't, she tried a different tack. "When did you and Noreen get married?"

"What do you mean when?"

"Before or after Chloe was born?" she whispered.

"After."

"After the paternity test?" Pepper asked, butting in despite her earlier insistence that she was here as a chaperone only.

"Yes."

Lila said, "It's understandable that you didn't wholly trust her."

"Noreen never forgave me for doubting her word."

Pepper said, "She used the pregnancy as bait, and when she caught you, she didn't like the fact that you married her because of your child. How twisted is that?"

"It's actually quite normal," Lila said. "Getting back to those rumors of affairs."

A fish jumped near the boat. Closer to shore, a bullfrog croaked. Letting the boat drift toward the dock, Joe finally said, "There was talk around McCaffrey's that she'd had an affair with the gardener. I couldn't prove it."

"How did you feel when she went after your father?"

"Oh, boy," Pepper muttered under her breath.

"How do you think I felt? How would you feel?" he asked loud enough to cause all of them to glance at the dark window in the cabin.

"How did you find out?" Lila whispered.

Lowering his voice again, he said, "Dad told me. There were witnesses, and he figured it was better if I heard it from him. Later, I heard he told Noreen what she could do with her slutty ways."

Joe's eyes were in shadow, but even in the dark she could tell that his face was fully engaged in his scowl. Last night Lila and Pepper had compared notes. All Pepper had received from Joe Sr. was a hint, but while Darci had been putting these godawful lowlights in Lila's hair, the sordid tales of Noreen's conquests had come tumbling out. The way Darci recalled it, Joe Sr. had told his daughter-in-law to go rub on somebody who cared.

"What did you do when your father told you?" Lila asked.

"I moved into the spare bedroom. I saw a financial planner and spoke with a divorce attorney."

"How long was that before Noreen disappeared?" Lila asked quietly.

"Ten months."

That seemed like a long time to Lila. "Had you begun divorce proceedings?"

"No."

"Why not?" Pepper asked.

The deep breath Joe took then slowly released held Pepper and Lila spellbound. Rowing again, he finally said, "Chloe begged me not to."

"Chloe knew?" Lila ducked her head, because this time her voice had carried across the water. "Who told her?"

Joe said, "Who told *you*? Word gets around."

"No wonder nobody seems to care whether Noreen is alive or dead," Pepper whispered.

"Chloe cares." Joe pulled on the oars with so much force the boat lunged toward shore.

Holding on tightly, Lila said, "Did Noreen have an affair with anyone other than your gardener?"

This time his hesitation was palpable. "An actual affair as compared to a flirtation? I just don't know."

"Somebody must know something," Lila whispered. Was it her imagination? Or had the curtain fluttered again? "Is anybody else in Murray missing?"

"Missing?"

"As in gone without a trace?" Lila whispered.

Joe stared into the darkness toward the orchard. "I was away a lot, but occasionally families move to Murray, and others move away. People retire to warmer climates, but the only other person who up and disappeared was Brenda Streeter, and that was seven years ago. Why?"

"It's just a feeling I have."

Pepper and Joe both waited for Lila to continue.

Finally, she said, "The woman you described was insecure, and an insecure woman doesn't leave one man until she has another one to go to."

"What happened after you heard rumors about Noreen and your gardener?"

"I fired his ass."

"Could she have run away with him?" Pepper whispered.

Joe shook his head. "He's still in the Valley."

"Are you sure Noreen wasn't seeing someone else?" Lila asked.

They'd reached the dock. At first Lila thought it was a coincidence that Joe busied himself steadying the boat while Pepper climbed out. Eventually it became apparent that he wasn't going to answer.

Pepper must have surmised as much, too. Rather than repeating the question, she slapped at another mosquito.

"Next time don't wear perfume," he said. "They're attracted to the scent."

"At least I'm attracting something."

"Are you leaving, too?" Joe asked Lila when she followed Pepper onto the dock.

"I have to wash my hair."

Waiting for her to fall into step, Pepper whispered drolly, "That was original."

"Did you notice he didn't answer when I asked if Noreen was seeing someone before she disappeared?" Lila whispered.

"I noticed."

They both turned around on the path. The three-quarter moon was reflected on the surface of the pond, but it didn't light upon Joe on the dock or on shore. He must have gone quietly inside. That was strange. In the past, he'd always let the door slam behind him.

"I wonder who he was thinking about when he chose not to answer your question," Pepper said, swatting and swearing with equal parts enthusiasm.

Lila didn't know, but she agreed with Pepper. Joe had had somebody in mind.

* * *

The central air-conditioning had been working overtime all evening, and so had Katherine. She was washing the big pots and pans that never came clean in the dishwasher when Heath brought his newspaper to the kitchen. The timer happened to ding while he was still there. Drying her hands, she took the pan of brownies out of the oven.

Sniffing appreciatively, he said, "Something smells good enough to eat."

It was what her daddy used to say, and hearing it again made the place behind her breastbone swell sweetly.

"What did you prepare tonight?" Heath asked.

He hadn't shaved since morning. He looked good spit and polished, but she'd always liked the slight stubble on his jaw. She turned away lest he see the flush on her cheeks. "Chicken fried steak and baby red potatoes and chocolate chunk fudge brownies."

"My mother used to make them," he said.

"It's your mama's recipe."

Silence.

"I'm taking it all to Lila's tomorrow."

"You've been cooking for her a lot lately."

"I cook for you, too."

"I know you do. I'm not complaining. It's good to see you enjoying something you love to do."

Her eyes watered. By the time she finally turned around, she was alone in the kitchen, and once again it was too late to broach the subject that kept them on their respective sides of the invisible line they'd drawn through their marriage.

She covered the food then arranged all the casserole dishes on the second shelf on the refrigerator where she would be able to grab them quickly tomorrow. She had a busy morning ahead of her at the store. An appraiser was coming down from New York, and Katherine planned to be at her best. Antiques were her life, after all.

She'd been perfecting her routine these past few weeks. She prepared food in the evenings, spent mornings at the store, dashed home long enough to heat everything, then loaded the dishes into sturdy baskets and carted everything to her car with just enough time to arrive and serve dinner at The Meadows. Goodness, she was almost as organized as Heath. She wondered when she'd adopted that trait.

She took her shower at ten o'clock as she always did. Cinching the sash of her robe tightly at her waist, she padded downstairs and tiptoed past the study to check one last time that the doors were locked and all burners off.

Heath came upstairs at eleven. She was tired enough to have fallen asleep immediately, but she lay awake listening to the pipes rumble, the shower door clank closed and eventually open. He used to sing in the shower, belting out tunes from old musicals. His favorites were *Oklahoma* and *Fiddler On The Roof*. She tried to remember when he'd stopped. How could she have failed to notice?

Finally, she heard the pad of his footsteps as he entered their room. She held perfectly still as he crawled in on his side. The bed shifted slightly beneath his weight. She could tell by the sound of his breathing that he was lying on his back.

"Are you asleep?" he asked in a husky whisper.

She could have feigned sleep, but she said, "No."

"I was thinking."

"About what?" she whispered.

"About chicken fried steak."

"You were thinking about chicken fried steak?" She wondered if he heard the smile in her voice. "What about it?"

"I haven't had that in years."

The house was so quiet suddenly that Katherine understood what a deafening silence meant. "Maybe you'd like to join us for dinner tomorrow," she said before she lost her nerve.

"At The Meadows?"

He meant at Joe's.

"Yes," she said.

"How do you think Lila would feel about that?"

He meant how would she feel about it.

"It's our food," she said, still facing the wall. "I don't see why you couldn't eat some of it."

Another long silence ensued.

At supper tonight she'd told him Chloe was home for two weeks. He'd asked how she was. It was the first time in two years either of them had mentioned a child. Katherine didn't tell Heath how much Chloe looked like Noreen, or how much she needed a mother. A lot of girls grew up without mothers. And a lot of women were perfectly content without children.

Why couldn't she be one of them?

She was trying to keep her marriage from gasping its last breath, and she and Heath didn't need painful reminders of what they didn't have. Lately, she'd been focusing on what they did have. Katherine had gone so far as to make a mental list.

They had a beautiful home, good standing in the community, a comfortable nest egg for retirement, good health. Since that seemed more like an advertisement for an investment company or stock portfolio, she'd gotten more creative. She was thankful for her store—how could she have failed to put that at the top of her list? And for her friends. Lila and Pepper were welcome additions, but she had old friends, too. She had hobbies, which included cooking. And she had an adventurous nature. Dancing in the moonlight without music qualified as an adventure, as well as what she was hoping to accomplish at The Meadows.

"Do you sit down at noon?" he finally asked.

Katherine swallowed. "I'll have Lila set another place." She wet her lips, and added, "Those three boys eat twice their weight every day. And Joe keeps up with them."

"In that case, I won't be late."

They both waited, breathing lightly, listening for the other to say more. Katherine didn't know what else to add and apparently neither did Heath. At least this was a start. For the first time in a long time, she fell asleep looking forward to tomorrow.

CHAPTER 12

The women were up to something, Joe thought as he dipped his brush into the white paint. Women usually were.

When Joe was fourteen, his father had tried to explain it to him. "There are three kinds of women, son," he'd said as he'd started the truck he was still driving today.

His father had picked him up from baseball practice, and Joe's mind had been on making it to the playoffs, but he'd wondered if his father was going to tell him that things were getting serious with Nancy Irish, the elementary schoolteacher he'd started seeing that spring.

"Some women believe they deserve losers, and losers are what they get. Others set their sights on the perfect man then proceed to try to mold him into what they want him to be."

No fourteen-year-old boy thought his old man was an expert on women, but there was something in his father's voice that took Joe's mind off baseball long enough to ask, "What's the third?"

His dad had started fiddling with the radio's reception.

"The third what?"

"You said there were three kinds of women."

"Oh." He looked into Joe's face and smiled. "Your mother was the third kind."

The conversation hadn't shed much light on the fairer sex, but it had reminded Joe that there were fine people in the world, and his mother had been one of them. Not that Joe pretended to understand human beings in general. Women were the relationship experts. Studying men was one of their more time-consuming pastimes. They analyzed a man's every word and move then discussed them with their friends. No wonder guys felt like slides under a microscope. It was the reason men ran in packs. There was safety in numbers.

Who was he kidding? Men weren't safe from women and most of them didn't care to be.

He loaded his paintbrush again, noting the way voices carried from every direction. It had been a hell of a lot quieter around here when Myrtle Ann was alive. Quieter, yes, but she was a woman, too, and had started all this. Joe couldn't bring himself to scowl, for no matter how much he tried to mind, he wasn't sorry about most of the changes Myrtle Ann had set in motion, for one of those changes was Lila's arrival.

He'd never met a more undemanding woman. She

never intentionally drew attention to herself, which meant there was another reason she was the first person he sought each time he drove into the driveway or left the cabin. She drew him without trying, inhabiting the farm by day and his dreams by night. Despite the fact that he woke up as tangled as his sheets, he was glad Lila was here, glad about most of the changes Myrtle Ann had initiated.

Heath's arrival for dinner was one exception. The invitation had to have been Katherine's doing. Whatever she was up to, she had her work cut out for her. Heath and Joe had sat at opposite ends of the table. Distance hadn't kept it from being damn awkward.

Dinner break usually lasted an hour. Since it was easier for Joe to keep busy than to pretend he didn't mind that Heath was here, he'd gone back to painting as soon as he'd finished eating.

Heath seemed to be experiencing his own problems. As the mayor, he surely knew how to appease little old ladies, charm voters and more often than not he outsmarted those who tried to take advantage of city hall. Yet he was no match for Lila, Pepper and Katherine, who'd surrounded him much the way they'd all surrounded the goats yesterday. He was helping Katherine carry the baskets containing the empty casserole dishes back to her trunk. He probably knew as well as Joe that it was no accident that the women herded him past the old Corvair Rusty was tinkering on. Of course he couldn't help taking a look, too. By the time Joe needed another gallon of paint, Katherine had driven away, Lila, Pepper and Chloe had settled on the porch, and there was grease halfway up Heath's forearms.

Since all Joe had left to paint on this side of the house was the porch, he put the can down at the far corner and got busy. From this angle he couldn't see Lila's face, but he heard her say, "Would you care for a glass of southern iced tea, Chloe?"

There was that snort again. "What's the difference between northern and southern iced tea, anyway?" she asked.

"Southern iced tea is sweet," Lila said affably.

"Like southern girls," Pepper added.

Joe could only imagine the face Chloe pulled. She stood up, swished her hair behind her shoulders and flounced off toward the orchard.

Lila said, "Pepper, for heaven's sake. You're supposed to be the adult."

"If she looks any farther down her nose she'll be cross-eyed. Right now, she thinks she's the only girl in the world who has issues. Let her sulk. I know how to handle her because I used to be like her."

"Used to be?" Joe couldn't help muttering under his breath.

Lila laughed out loud. "What about you, Joe?"

"Guys don't sulk. We—"

"Invade foreign countries," Pepper said for him.

Still smiling, Lila said, "Would you care for a glass of iced tea? Or are you sweet enough, too?"

In plain view now, he said, "Never developed a taste for it. Nice hat."

"You like it?" she asked, tugging at the bill of the ball cap she'd discovered on the newel post on the back porch when she woke up this morning. "Do you think you should go after Chloe?"

Joe looked toward the orchard. "Is this behavior normal?"

"There's a wide range of what is considered normal. She's been through a great deal. Have you tried to talk to her about whatever is bothering her? About her mother?"

"She doesn't want to talk about Noreen."

"Have you suggested she visit a counselor?"

Sweat beaded on his forehead and slowly trickled down the sides of his face. "She wouldn't talk to the child psychologists, either."

"I'm telling both of you," Pepper grumbled, "she just needs to sulk. For some of us, it's good for the soul."

But Lila was on another tack. "Are you saying Chloe never talks about her mother?"

"I don't remember the last time." Joe wiped his brow with the back of his hand.

"That's unusual," Lila said thoughtfully. "Girls whose mothers have died normally want to talk about them all the time. Of course, she doesn't know if her mother is alive or not."

"Maybe she believes Noreen deserted her," Pepper said.

"I think she's afraid I did it." Joe was tired of everything always coming back to Noreen's disappearance, tired of trying to make sense of it, tired of thinking about it.

"You told her you didn't harm Noreen, didn't you?"

"What do you think?"

"I take it she didn't believe you," Pepper said.

"Why wouldn't Chloe believe you?" Lila asked.

"Because actions speak louder than words."

"What did she see?" Lila asked quietly.

"I never laid a hand on Noreen, but sometimes Chloe could see how difficult it was not to."

"Did anybody else see that?" Lila asked.

"My father did."

"Where does he think Noreen went?"

"You'll have to ask *him*."

Joe was so busy looking at Lila he forgot Pepper was still there until she said, "I'm going to need to take the car."

"Of course," Lila said. "But—"

Pepper rushed inside, emerging again almost immediately, tall, cool and svelte in aqua capris and a matching sleeveless top. "Don't wait up!" she called, and with a wave and a honk of the horn, she was gone.

"Wasn't she wearing shorts before?" Joe asked.

Nodding, Lila thought she'd caught a whiff of Pepper's perfume, too. "She seemed eager to go into town."

"Any idea why?" he asked, returning to his painting.

"She's going to see a man."

"How do you know?"

"It's just a feeling," she said.

Their eyes met.

"A strong feeling?" he asked.

She smiled. It was coming back, different than before, but every bit as life-affirming.

Chloe saw the middle Streeter boy ambling along the path. Hidden in the branches of her favorite apple tree, she waited until he was directly below her. "Where do you think you're going?"

He dropped to a crouch, cowering, his arms flying upward to protect his face. When he recovered enough to look up, she was sorry she'd scared him. He and his younger brother had brown hair, cheap clothes and poor manners. This one had old man's eyes. Without saying a word, he started back the way he'd come.

"Do you climb trees?" she called.

Shoulders stiff, he said, "What's it to you if I do?" Now he sounded like every other boy she'd ever known.

"Come on up."

He seemed frozen in indecision. She didn't know why she cared. After all, he was dirty. He was only eleven. And he was poor. Normally, three strikes meant O-U-T out.

"Unless you're afraid of heights. Then don't come up, because it's pretty high up here."

She had to hide her smile this time, because her ploy worked. Boys were so predictable.

After choosing a branch higher than hers, he said, "I didn't know girls like you climbed trees."

Girls like her?

She was trying to decide if she should feel insulted when he said, "My little brother fell asleep in the shade by the barn. I'm supposed to be watchin' him, so I can't stay up here long."

She wondered why someone as young as he was had such so much responsibility. "Why isn't your mother watching him? Is she at work?"

"She run off." He picked a handful of leaves then watched them sift to the ground.

"She left you and your brothers?"

"When Ricky was one. He don't remember her at all. I barely do."

Chloe didn't know why her throat almost closed up, or why she said, "What do you remember about her?"

He shrugged one shoulder. For a second she was sidetracked by the dirty streak on his face and the grime on his hands.

"Do you remember what your mother looks like?" she asked.

"Do you remember what yours looks like?"

She was thirteen and was getting the best private education money could buy. How had he managed to slip that question past her defenses? "Of course I do. My mother's only been gone for two years. Plus I have pictures."

"You're lucky. My dad burned all my mom's pictures."

"Why would he do that?" she asked.

Ryan looked away, and something told her not to ask him again.

"I think she might have looked like Miz Avery."

Chloe had known Katherine Avery all her life. Katherine was a southern lady who was educated in the arts and in the finer things in life. Chloe doubted that Ryan Streeter's mother would have had very much in common with such a woman. "Why do you think that?" she asked.

"Miz Avery smells good, like something cookin'.

Sometimes it shoots through me that my mom smelled good, too. You know, the kind of good that fills your belly when it's empty and makes you feel safe."

Tears gathered in Chloe's eyes because Ryan Streeter was lucky if his mother had done that. "You remember her," she said around the lump in her throat. "You might not know it, but you remember. I'll bet you're right. I'll bet she was just as pretty as Katherine."

"Yeah?"

"Yeah."

Chloe was feeling pretty good about herself. It wasn't so bad talking to someone less fortunate.

"Just so you know," Ryan said, "Rusty doesn't like it when girls make goo-goo eyes at him."

She did a double take. "Why are you telling me?"

"Why do you think?"

It bothered her that she was so transparent, but she couldn't help asking, "Do a lot of girls make eyes at him?"

"Girls are always trying to get him to notice them. My dad told him girls are only good for one thing. I can't repeat what else he said." Just like that, he started to climb down.

"Where are you going?"

"I better check on Ricky." He swung from a low branch then dropped to the ground.

"Hey, Ryan?"

Retrieving his ball cap from the tall grass, he said, "What?"

"Your dad's wrong."

"I know."

She waited a few seconds. When she couldn't see him, she said, "Know what else? You're smarter than you look."

"You're nicer than you look," he called back.

Chloe wasn't accustomed to being bested by a younger boy in secondhand clothes. It wasn't long before she heard him calling to his little brother. She stayed where she was, hidden in the branches of her favorite apple tree. She liked it up here, and thought she could just stay here forever. Up here, she could pretend that she was like all her friends at school, that she was going to Europe with her family this summer, that everybody didn't wonder about her in the back of their minds. Mostly, she could pretend that her father had loved her mother. And that her mother had loved her.

"You're in my way."

Pepper moved to one side of the storeroom's doorway. When Joe Sr. shouldered past her she bit her lip to stifle her smile because no matter what he thought, his grumpiness wasn't off-putting. "Can I help carry anything?"

He didn't bother answering.

It had rankled when Katherine and Lila had assumed she was helpless. Today, she found it oddly amusing. It was more fun than spy work. In the old spy spoof movie she'd watched last night, the unkempt P.I. had told his new sidekick that surveillance was ninety-nine percent boredom, but that last one percent made up for it. She'd thought about that as she'd checked out the people in McCaffrey's when she'd arrived. Once again, the place wasn't exactly hopping. "Why do you suppose The General Lee does a better business than McCaffrey's?"

"McCaffrey's does all right."

Finally, a rise out of him. "Who wants to be all right when they could be extraordinary?"

He grunted an answer before turning his back on her. Since he was facing the mirror behind the bar, she climbed onto the bar stool where she had the best view of his reflection. "The place is on life support. I find myself wanting to yell 'clear', and zap it with paddles."

A pained look crossed his features, as if all this idle chatter was giving him a headache. It wasn't as if she'd intentionally set out to give him a headache. She'd tried asking him about Joe and Noreen. Was it her fault he didn't keep up his end of the conversation?

How long could it take to arrange the Captain Morgan next to the Jack Daniel's? She'd been at McCaffrey's for forty-five minutes. He'd been avoiding her question for forty-four.

Do you have any idea who Noreen might have been having an affair with, any idea at all?

The place reeked of smoke. Pushing an ashtray containing a smoldering cigarette closer to Bud Streeter, she wrinkled up her nose and said, "You may not have heard, but secondhand smoke can kill you."

"Everybody's gotta die of something," Bud said.

Why did his laugh always turn her stomach? Preferring to speak to Joe, she said, "Do you think your daughter-in-law is dead?"

His hesitation was barely noticeable. "What difference does it make what I think?"

He leaned over to pick something up, and she got a good look at his rear end. He looked a lot younger from this angle. The rest of him wasn't bad, either, a little older than her usual conquests, perhaps, but not bad.

Whoa. This ornery, two-bit, information withholding, annoying man who was old enough to be her father was not a conquest. He seemed younger than her father, though. "How old are you?" she heard herself ask.

"Old enough to know better," Bud said on another derogatory laugh. "Ain't that what you told Noreen, Pop?"

Pepper swallowed her distaste. Pasting on a saccharine smile, she said, "Did she ever come on to you, Bud?"

His whisker stubble didn't quite conceal the pits

in his face. He took a long drag on his cigarette, exhaling smoke into her face as he said, "You think she went slumming? Would you?"

She jumped when Joe Sr. slammed a drink down in front of her. "McCaffrey's is for paying customers. Either drink up or go to a coffee shop."

He may have sounded ornery, but she knew when she'd just been rescued. Taking a sip of her beer, she said, "Why isn't Joe Jr. here yet?"

"He has the next two weeks off to spend with Chloe."

"You're short-handed?"

"I ran the place by myself for years."

"You were younger then." She could see she'd scraped a nerve. "Since you haven't told me how old you are, I must surmise that you're no spring chicken. Running a tavern day and night must be a lot for one person."

"I don't have anything better to do." He poured another beer and handed it to a paying customer.

"That's a crying shame." She tried to decide what to call him. "Joe" didn't seem quite right, and she couldn't bring herself to call him Pops, as everyone else did. She tried Joseph out in her mind before trying it on him. "Joseph."

He looked at her, and didn't immediately look away.

"Hey, Pop!" somebody yelled. "What's it take to get another round back here?"

If Pepper had believed in aliens, she would have

insisted one had taken over her body. Why else did she slide off her stool and slip behind the bar? "Move over, Joseph. First, show me what to do."

"You ever tend bar?"

"Not formally."

"You ever mixed a drink?" he asked.

"My father likes his martinis shaken, not stirred."

Up close she saw that his eyes were lighter brown than his son's. The silver at his temples gave him a wizened look that seemed premature all of a sudden.

"This isn't a martini crowd." The harder he tried to be gruff, the less grouchy he was sounding all the time.

"I hadn't noticed." She winked, then set about filling five beer glasses from the tap, scraped off the suds, and carried the entire tray to a back table.

"Looks like you're gonna get lucky yet, Pops," Bud said loud enough for everybody in the place to hear.

Bud Streeter's laugh came straight from the gutter. Once again it raised goose bumps up and down Pepper's spine.

"Did I tell you Lila's friend has taken a job at Mc-Caffrey's?" Heath asked. "It's the talk of the town."

Even though Katherine hadn't heard him come into the kitchen, she didn't jump. Lately, the atmosphere had become less charged with friction. That alone was cause for celebration.

"Pepper is adventurous, I'll give her that." Katherine spoke into the refrigerator where she was putting tomorrow's dinner away for safekeeping. "I really think she's going to be good for Chloe. She seems to understand that girl. They certainly have a lot in common. Did you know that Pepper attended Chloe's boarding school when she was Chloe's age?"

Katherine noticed that she and Heath often began conversations with *did I tell you* and *did you know?* As if either of them would have forgotten they hadn't spoken of anything of importance in a long time. At least they'd started talking again. Neither of them had broached any difficult subjects, and they certainly hadn't ventured across the invisible line they'd been living with, but comfortable conversation was preferable to polite recitals of their respective days.

She'd taken a deep breath before she'd brought up Chloe the first time. Since he'd seemed comfortable with it, she'd let herself continue. "I swear I never know what's going to come out of that girl's mouth," she said. "I remember when my mama used to say that about me. Last summer, Chloe was still a little girl. Now, I see signs of a woman lurking. Joe had better be paying attention. This is the time in a girl's life when she can really start down the wrong path."

She knew Heath was still in the room, because every once in a while he grunted something to let her know he was listening. Feeling self-conscious suddenly, she said, "I don't believe you've mentioned what your schedule is like for tomorrow."

Regaining a level of self-control, she reached across the table to bundle up the newspaper he'd carried in with him. Instead of finishing the task, she remained standing on one side of the table; he remained standing on the other side.

For the past two years this marred Pennsylvania-made table might as well have been the ocean, the chairs opposite shores. She loved the ocean, but not in this context. Her parents used to take her and her sister to the ocean every spring. Then it had seemed vast and powerful, a living, breathing, swelling body that sustained every sort of life form from the creatures living in it to those making their living on it. This ocean in her kitchen wasn't majestic or life-sustaining. It was simply vast and empty. Lately, the shores seemed closer, though.

"Tomorrow?" he said. And she swore he had to drag his eyes away from her mouth. "I have a light schedule, so I thought I'd drive over to Staunton and check on some used engine parts for Rusty's car."

"Do you think you can help him get it running?"

He made one of those sounds men made when they believed something went without saying. "If

Chester's has them, I thought I'd bring the parts with me tomorrow."

"You're going back to The Meadows tomorrow?" she asked, breathless.

"If it's all right."

"It isn't all right."

"Oh. In that case—"

"It's better than all right." In her haste to reassure him, it was possible she went too far. Slowing down, she said, "I think it's good, what you're doing for Rusty. He's never had a mentor. His only example has come from Bud. It'll be a miracle if all three of those boys don't end up in the juvenile court system before they're grown. What's after that? Prison?" She carried the newspapers to the butler's pantry.

Behind her, Heath said, "The two little ones look up to Rusty. As long as he's okay, I think they will be. He's smart. He remembers where every engine part he removes goes and how it works. It takes a knack."

He continued talking about engines, and Katherine's mind drifted to Chloe and all the things she wanted to do with the girl while she was here these two weeks.

"By the way," Heath said before returning to the study.

"Yes?"

"What's for dinner?"

"Dinner?"

"Tomorrow. I was just wondering so I'll know what to look forward to."

"Beef tips in mushroom gravy over buttered noodles, sugar snap peas, and chocolate chunk fudge brownies." She looked at him, thinking *the way to a man's heart...*

Was that what she was doing? Finding a way to Heath's heart?

Or was she finding a way to hers?

CHAPTER 13

How could Lila have thought she needed quiet?

What she'd needed was this calibration of calamity, this free-for-all chorus of voices raised just to be heard, of questions that often went half-answered, and hungers that were never assuaged for long.

And that was just dinner.

How quickly she'd adjusted to referring to the noon meal in that manner. Sometimes, she thought she heard the soft cadence of a southern accent creeping into her speech. She was like her mother's hothouse hibiscus, except she didn't need to be taken inside in winter. Like the garden plants outside the kitchen window, her roots were sinking deep into the red Virginia soil while her mind, body and soul unfurled, thriving in the heat and humidity.

Lila wasn't the only one growing stronger. She'd noticed a sheen of purpose in Pepper's eyes lately that hadn't been there before. Perhaps having her purse strings clipped hadn't been a bad thing after all. There was something different about Katherine, too. Each day she served something delicious on her grand-mother's Wedgwood platter or in one of her mama's Worcester porcelain bowls or some other piece that had meaning and history. Today, she'd presented them all with beef barley soup in Heath's great-aunt's wedding tureen. How Katherine managed to transport the soup without spilling it was a mystery to Lila. But then, so was Katherine.

Lila had set nine places today. Heath and Katherine were here, of course, and Joe's father had stopped by to see Chloe. Since Pepper was opening the tavern, Joe Sr. sat where she normally did. The antique pedestal table stretched out like the floating bridge Lila had come across while meandering the countryside the other day. Heath sat beside his wife, as far from Joe as either man could physically manage without leaving the table. Thanks to Katherine, the Streeter brothers were learning to hold their forks properly and keep their elbows off the table. There were fewer hollows in the boys' faces and fewer shadows in their eyes. In Joe's eyes, too, Lila realized when their fingers met around the basket of rolls he passed her. It was just a look, certainly no more than that, and yet in it was a connection, an awareness, the feeling that she was coming home after an exhausting trip to someplace she no longer needed to be. He hadn't kissed her again, but she knew he would. Last night Lila had fallen asleep in the middle of an old *Gunsmoke* rerun, and she'd dreamed Joe was Matt Dillon and Lila was Miss Kitty, and everything about their feelings for each other was conveyed in searing glances over a bottle of whiskey. Lila woke up relieved that it was the present day, and certain she wouldn't be satisfied forever with searing glances.

Gradually the clatter of dishes and the rise and fall of voices penetrated her dreamy abstraction. She glanced away and caught Chloe looking at her. The girl didn't return Lila's smile.

"Would y'all care for more bread pudding?" Katherine always knew when to come to everybody's rescue.

Lila took a helping of the old-fashioned vanilla-laced dessert, smothered it with real whipped cream, then passed it on to Ryan and Ricky, who were talking about the yearly shearing of the Angora goats. Mimicking Ned Pearson, who'd stayed after the shearing this morning, Ricky hooked his thumbs around make-believe suspenders and said, "Buck looks like a mountain man who just stepped out of his spring bath."

Even Chloe smiled, for it *had* been a pretty good imitation.

"Speaking of baths," Katherine said, pinning Ricky with her gaze, "Ms. Delaney has graciously offered the use of her bathtub. I expect you to fill it with warm water, and I don't want to see you again until every inch of you has been scrubbed clean. Use the washcloth I laid out, and the soap and shampoo, and the scrub brush if you have to."

Seeing Ryan slinking toward the door, she said, "Don't go far, because you're next, young man."

While Ricky trudged to the bathroom to do as she commanded, Katherine turned to Rusty. "I want you to take these leftovers home."

"Yes 'um."

She said something to Joe, too, but it was handled so quietly all Lila heard was Joe's reply, which sounded a lot like Rusty's had. Chloe took her grandfather outside to show him the goats, and Joe went with them.

After everyone else had scattered, Katherine ran the sink full of hot, sudsy water. Watching an iridescent bubble float up, Lila said, "Is there a difference between a married man and a man who happens to still be married?"

Katherine turned her head slowly, but made no reply. Lila knew the answer. "I need to find Noreen, Katherine." For Joe's sake, for Chloe's sake, and for hers.

But how did you find a woman who was either dead or didn't want to be found?

"Have you ever been attracted to an older man, Lila?"

At first Lila thought she'd heard wrong. Pepper stared despondently across the pond, perspiration glistening at the base of her throat and upper lip. She hadn't moved in so long Lila had begun to wonder if she'd fallen asleep behind her Louis Vuitton sunglasses.

Letting the water she'd scooped up trickle between her fingers, Lila said, "Define older."

"Old enough to be Joe's father."

Pepper and Joseph McCaffrey Sr.? Thank goodness Lila no longer blurted whatever she was thinking. "I can't say I have. What's going on? Are you two talking? Are you seeing him? Is he a nice guy?"

"Are you kidding? He's obstinate, he's curt, he's critical and he's glib."

"I can see why you're attracted to him."

"I knew you'd understand."

Before either of them knew it, they were both laughing. Sometimes Lila wondered if there was something in the water here, because she never used to laugh like this.

Katherine drove up while they were recovering. "What's going on?" she asked.

"I'm having a heatstroke."

"Funny, I heard you have a thing for Joe Sr."

Pepper jolted to her feet, her hands finding her damp cheeks. "Who told you that?"

"Trudy told Ginny Calhoun, who told Irene Motz, who told Priscilla Darby, who told me after she purchased another of Myrtle Ann's pieces." She handed

Lila a check for a substantial amount of money. "I forget who told Trudy."

That lineup sounded vaguely familiar to Lila.

"I didn't see Joe's truck when I drove in," Katherine said while Pepper was still flabbergasted. "Is Chloe here?"

"Joe went up to Weyers Cave to check on some used parts for Rusty's car. Chloe is in the cabin instant messaging her friends."

"I picked up a few items for her." Katherine rattled the shopping bag in her right hand. "I can't wait to show her."

After she'd slipped inside, Pepper shook her head. "Is it just me, or does she try too hard with that child?"

Katherine was smitten with the girl, Lila suspected with all girls. In return, Chloe was polite but standoffish with her. Just this afternoon, Katherine had been putting baskets with sturdy handles in her trunk when Chloe had traipsed by. "You're just the girl I wanted to talk to," Katherine had exclaimed.

"Why?"

Try as she might, Katherine hadn't been able to entice Chloe to spend the afternoon with her at the store. While Katherine's smile was still wavering, Ryan Streeter had skipped down the porch steps, his hair still damp from his recent bath. "I'll go!"

Katherine had looked perplexed, but both Ryan

and Ricky had been radiant as they'd ridden away in Katherine's car.

Now, here Katherine was, trying again with Chloe.

The screen door opened and quietly closed. Sensing Katherine's dejection, Lila called, "How did she like her gifts?"

Katherine shrugged.

Fanning herself with a piece of cardboard, Pepper said, "You know how girls this age are when it comes to their friends."

"I suppose you're right." Katherine didn't sound convinced.

"Do you know what I think?" Lila asked.

"Do we need Tarot cards for this?" Pepper asked drolly.

"Very funny. I think we need to have a little fun."

"Sorry, I'm out of mint julep."

"Who feels like swimming?" Lila asked.

"It's too hot to walk all the way back to the big house for my swimsuit," Pepper said. "What I wouldn't do for a breeze."

"I didn't bring my swimsuit," Katherine said. "I'll just leave you two al—"

"Who said anything about swimsuits?" Lila toed out of her espadrilles.

"You must be joking!" Pepper and Katherine said at the same time.

"Don't tell me neither of you has ever gone skinny-dipping."

"Please," Pepper said. "I've spent entire summers in the French Riviera."

Lila stuck out her tongue at her friend and shimmied out of her shorts. Her shirt came next, followed by her bra and panties.

"It's still broad daylight!" Katherine exclaimed.

"No one else can see us." Lila screeched when the water reached key places, then dove under, surfacing the way otters did at the zoo. "This is amazing!" she called. "Joe says it's spring-fed. I say it's heaven. It's nature's air-conditioning. Are you going to stand there and watch?"

Pepper was the first to move. "Come on, Katherine. Lila's right." Her sandals landed nearby, the rest of her clothes a cushion for her sunglasses, her first yelp every bit as playful as Lila's had been.

There was something about the spontaneity of their laughter and the occasional glimpse of bare flesh that caused Katherine's heart to feel as if it was beating too slowly. In comparison, she felt staid and proper, brittle. Old. Something inside her was trying to scream, and yet she remained rooted to the spot, barely breathing, barely living.

What had she become?

All the commotion brought Chloe outside. "What

are they doing?" She eyed the clothes strewn on the grass. "Oh, my God, are they skinny-dipping?"

"As a matter of fact, they are."

"Are you getting in?"

"Me?" Katherine wondered if the girl could hear the beat of her heart.

Suddenly, she saw herself at Chloe's age, being taught about china patterns and etiquette, making plans for every step of her future right down to when she would marry and what she would name her first daughter. Each time she'd set another plan in stone, she'd doused the spark of wildfire born in her. She'd been so intent upon growing up and achieving her goals she'd forgotten to be young.

Chloe giggled at the spectacle of Lila's rump surfacing before the rest of her. The pure joy in that sweet giggle split something open inside Katherine.

"Are you two prim and proper southern belles going to stand there gawking? Or are you going to have a little fun?"

Katherine's heart sped up. Her face flamed. And somewhere deep inside her, the silent scream turned into a spark of something all but forgotten.

Everyone was surprised when she shed her clothes at the water's edge, but no one was more truly shocked than Katherine herself. She walked into the shallows, a woman on a mission, dove under, and came up, a girl on the brink of discovery.

"Are you okay?" Lila asked, swimming closer.

"No. But I think I'm going to be."

"Attagirl."

They looked back when they heard a splash, and grinned at the girlish whoop that followed. Chloe swam past, her hair tied back in a scrunchie, her arms and legs strong and lean. When she grinned, Lila caught a glimpse of the little girl in the photograph Joe carried in his wallet, and she knew it wasn't too late for any of them.

They took turns showing off and performing various water acrobatics. Mostly they giggled and made outrageous wishes. When they grew tired, they started for shore. Once they could touch bottom, they walked four abreast, squeegeeing the water out of their eyes.

Thigh deep, Chloe was the first to notice the two men standing in the grass. She screamed and dropped to a crouch, submerged to her armpits. Lila slowed at first sight of the imposing figures. Katherine froze.

But Pepper kept right on walking. Scooping up her clothes, sandals and sunglasses on her way by, she held them close to her body as she strolled past Joe and Heath, who'd gallantly turned their backs.

Passing close by them on her way back to the big house, she said, "Don't tell your father I'm not a natural blonde. I want him to find out for himself."

Heath and Joe stared after her dazedly for a moment then automatically turned around. Instantly, Chloe screamed again.

"Damn," Heath said, choosing the lesser of two evils. "Talk about being between a rock and a hard place."

Joe and Heath stared at one another. They weren't friends. They weren't teammates. They were something far more elemental. They were both men.

"My father saw me naked. I'm never showing my face again." Chloe was sitting in the fresh straw, fully clothed now, gently petting the female goats.

Although Lila hadn't made a sound, she wasn't surprised Chloe had known she'd entered the barn. The girl had good instincts. Normally, Katherine would have insisted upon speaking with Chloe, but she had more important things to discuss with Heath, although it didn't look to Lila as if Heath had talking on his mind. Since Chloe had been mortified her father had seen her naked, Joe and Lila had decided it might be best if she spoke with her first.

"Do you believe black cats are bad luck?" Chloe asked.

"Not at all."

"What about werewolves?"

"What about them?" Lila asked, coming closer.

"Do you think they're real?"

"Not really."

"What about aliens?" the girl asked.

"I don't know, Chloe."

"What about mermaids? What about God?"

Lila tried to decide how to answer without sounding preachy. "I believe in God and in goodness. I suppose the existence of mermaids is possible. Who knows?"

"Maybe Atlantis really existed," Chloe said. She still hadn't looked at Lila. "Maybe mermaids are the only survivors."

The girl had a very good imagination. "That's an interesting theory."

"If there is a God, why do bad things happen?"

"That's an age-old question, Chloe." Lila had asked herself that same thing dozens of times after she'd been flogged on national television. "Whether we like it or not, bad things happen sometimes. I don't know why."

Chloe took a while to consider that. "The goats look embarrassed without their wooly coats," she said sadly. "Especially the fat one."

Lila sank to her knees in the loose straw and looked at the animals. Staring into eyes so black she couldn't see the pupils, she said, "Mo and Curly didn't like the electric clippers, but they're much cooler now."

Chloe reeled around. "How do you know that? Oh, my gosh, you really are the goat whisperer."

"Is that what they call me?" Lila asked, amused.

"Ricky Streeter does."

"Curly isn't fat, Chloe. She's going to have a baby." Now that she'd been sheared, it was obvious. Lila had been told the animal was too old to have more kids.

"Do you think it's Buck's?" Chloe asked.

Normally, little children asked a hundred questions. Not thirteen-year-old girls. "Since he's the only male around here, that would be my guess."

"You don't always know who the father is."

Somehow Lila didn't think they were talking about the goats. Oh, my God, she thought. "Chloe, you're not—"

The girl looked disgusted. "I'm thirteen. I go to an all girls' school. I haven't even been kissed, and everything else is gross."

Lila began to relax.

"What about you?" Chloe asked.

So much for relaxing.

"Are you and my dad, you know, sleeping together?"

Unable to hide her surprise, Lila said, "I think you should talk to your father about this."

"Meaning you are?"

"No. We're not. I think he's a fine man, but, well, anyway, we're not." Such eloquence. And to think she'd haled from one of the finest universities in the country.

Chloe stared at her as if trying to decide if she believed her. Her eyes were big and brown, her nose slightly upturned. The spattering of freckles across her cheeks made her look innocent. With her colt legs and corn-silk hair, she really was a pretty girl.

"What are you thinking?" she asked. "That I look like my mother?"

Actually, that was what Lila had been thinking. "You're beautiful, like her photograph, but you have your father's smile. Or should I say his scowl?"

The answer seemed to satisfy her. "You don't have any children, do you?"

Lila shook her head.

"What about brothers and sisters?"

"Like you, I'm an only child."

It occurred to Lila that she didn't know very much about thirteen-year-old girls. When she expected Chloe to sputter, she didn't. When she expected her to continue, she stared into the shadows as if she were seeing something else entirely.

"Dad said he took you to our house."

It was the perfect example of the last thing Lila expected Chloe to say. "Yes, he did."

"How did it look?"

Feeling as though she was finally getting to the heart of what was bothering Chloe, Lila said, "It was beautiful. Have you ever thought about asking your father to take you there?"

"And do what?"

"What do you want to do?"

Chloe drew her mouth to one side. "Do you think he would go?"

"I believe he would do just about anything in the world for you."

As if coming to her senses, Chloe said, "None of it matters because I'm never looking him in the eyes again."

The hair around Chloe's face was drying. Fighting the impulse to smooth the flyaway strands off her forehead, Lila said, "He's already seen you naked, you know."

"I was a baby, and that doesn't count."

"It could have been worse. He could have brought Rusty back with him."

Chloe's eyes opened wide and her front teeth came down on her lower lip. A moment later she giggled behind her hand. "You're right. It would have been worse. And it might have even gotten his attention."

Something told Lila this girl was going to turn a

lot of heads, and it was going to begin soon. "Your father is waiting for you at the cabin."

Chloe pulled a face.

"You might as well get it over with."

She looked at Lila's outstretched hand. After that brief hesitation, she took it, allowing Lila to help her up. "I'd rather go by myself. If I get too embarrassed, I'll just remember how Daddy looked at you."

Lila almost felt sorry for Joe. He didn't stand a chance against this girl.

Katherine's hands were still shaking when she unfastened her seat belt and turned off her car. Heath had already parked and was waiting for her at their back door, the epitome of calm.

She was glad they'd driven separately, but sorry she'd only had two miles to get her thoughts in order. Unfortunately her thoughts weren't in order because she'd spent the entire drive remembering the expression on Heath's face as he'd watched her plod out of the pond.

Flustered, she dropped her keys at the back door. They both bent down to pick them up. Her fingers curled around the keys. His curled around her hand. She was relieved when he released her, but nothing compared to the relief she felt when he retreated into the study to read his paper as he did every evening.

At least something was still normal.

She turned at the sound of his footsteps behind her. Swallowing a rising panic, she said, "Was something wrong with your newspaper?"

He stared at her, advancing slowly, surely, determinedly. "I can't stop thinking about the way you looked rising out of that water, the setting sun glistening on your wet skin, on your breasts, your waist, your belly, your thighs."

"Heath."

Everything about him was so familiar, the crease in one cheek, the shallow cleft in his chin, the breadth of his shoulders, the huskiness of his voice as he said, "Now that I've seen you naked again, I won't be able to keep from doing this."

If he hadn't kissed her at that precise moment, she might have been able to salvage her sensibility, to straighten her backbone and stiffen her upper lip. But his mouth came down on hers, and all her lips were capable of doing was softening, parting, accepting the intimacy of something beautiful and fleeting.

Tears were in her eyes when he lifted his face from hers. Despite his bravado, there was a flicker of uncertainty in his, as well.

"My mama told me to never let a man see me naked," she whispered.

His grin took her back to the early days of their marriage. His next kiss took her breath.

He unbuttoned his shirt, removed his tie, then moved on to help her out of her blouse. She gasped at the brush of his fingertips when he started unfastening her buttons.

"Don't worry. We're going to take this real slow."

"Heath, I don't know about this."

"Then I'll show you."

"Let's at least go upstairs."

"I like right here just fine. I'd take you on the front porch. Hell, I'd make love to you on the steps at city hall."

"You'd get arrested."

"It would be worth it."

She was glad he didn't say he'd already been in prison these last few years.

"Don't think," he said, lowering the zipper on her slacks.

It was as if he'd read her mind.

"What, pray tell, would you rather I do?"

When he told her, her eyes widened.

"Heath," she said on a gasp a short time later. "I thought you wanted to take this slow."

"We'll take it slow the second time." He kissed her long and hard and deep. "Or maybe the third."

CHAPTER 14

Pepper thought about Lila and Katherine as she drove into Murray Friday evening. More specifically, she thought about the way Joe and Heath had looked at Lila and Katherine at the water's edge earlier. The men had practically sizzled. She almost wished Joseph would have been there.

She'd always believed she needed city lights in order to find excitement. It was amazing the places a person could find excitement if she was looking. She was becoming philosophical. She was also late for work.

A week ago it had been easy to find a parking space near McCaffrey's Tavern. Tonight, she'd driven around the block three times before finally locating an empty place in the alley out back. Music played from the jukebox, and the pool table rarely sat idle. The regulars still came, but new people sauntered in and sat down beside them. They'd kept Pepper and Joseph hopping all week.

Did he appreciate her help?

He barely gave her the time of day. She'd been

under the impression he hadn't noticed she was a woman, certainly not of the living, breathing, bedding variety, but if the gossips in Murray knew it, he knew it, too. He just wasn't admitting it.

Now wasn't that interesting?

She arranged the mixed drinks and draft beers on her tray, and with a wink, set off to deliver them. She laughed at the customers' jokes, parlayed them with her own brand of wit, and pocketed their tips. Every so often she had to remove a stray hand from her rear end. And every so often she caught Joseph looking at her.

She didn't believe in the notion of soul mates. That was Lila's department, but Pepper had experienced this type of connection often enough to recognize a mutual attraction when it was staring her in the face. Prior to this summer, she wouldn't have even considered acting upon it. Prior to this summer, she wouldn't have gotten dirt under her fingernails, survived without air-conditioning, or touched up her own roots, either. There was something to be said for living authentically.

During a lull, she joined Joseph on the other side of the bar. "Busy night," she said, leaning on her elbows.

"This keeps up, I'm going to have to hire more waitstaff."

He was surveying the room, but she wasn't fooled. He was completely aware of her proximity.

"You're saying I'm good for business."

"I didn't say any such thing."

"All these people aren't coming just to see me. They're here to see what's happening between us."

At least she had his attention.

"Why, Joseph, you just checked me out." Surely God gave men Adam's apples just so women would know when they were trying to hide a reaction. She touched his cheek with three fingers then sauntered away to take another table's orders. Half the people in McCaffrey's saw the exchange and the other half had heard about it by last call. Despite her aching feet, Pepper had enjoyed the night immensely.

"You know," she said after he'd locked the back door, "the only two people who aren't happy about the boom in business are you and Bud Streeter, and he wouldn't be happy if he was hanged with a new rope. What does that mean, anyway? Why would anyone be happier to be hanged with a new rope than an old one?"

He had that pained look again, as if she was giving him a headache, so she stopped talking. When something scuttled behind the trash can, disappearing into the shadows beyond the mercury light's reach, she automatically stepped closer to him.

She could have easily melted into his side, but his stiff bearing didn't invite intimacy.

"What was her name?" she asked softly.

"Who?"

"Joe's mother."

Clearly, he hadn't expected that. "What difference does it make?"

Maybe she'd been away from civilization too long. Why else would she want to get to know such a man as Joseph McCaffrey Sr.? "You were young when she died."

"Everybody's young once."

"Stay with me here, Pops. You were young when you married, too. What were you, ten?"

The twitch at the corner of his mouth was gratifying.

"Fifteen?"

"We were both eighteen."

She did the mental math, and liked the answer. That meant he was still in his fifties. What a relief. "Was she—"

"No, she wasn't pregnant. Back then good girls didn't, at least not most of them. Why the hell am I telling you this?"

"That's a good question. Why are you telling me this? If I'm reading this wrong, say so."

His silence spoke volumes.

"She died when Joe was what, six? You've been alone for a long time."

"She was my first. I never said she was my last."

"So there have been others since. It's nice to know you haven't forgotten how, although I'm told it's like riding a bike."

He assumed a stance she'd seen his son adopt, one hand on his hip, the other one kneading the back of his neck. "I'm tired and you're trouble."

"Joseph?" she whispered close to his ear. "You're not that tired."

He took her keys and unlocked her car and saw that she got in. Just before closing her door, he said, "Her name was Penny."

She had to let the irony sink in. "That's priceless. At least you won't have to worry about calling out the wrong name in the heat of passion."

She watched him absorb the implications. "Pepper is short for Penelope?"

"Quite a coincidence, isn't it?"

His half smile was all male. "Do I get a say in any of this?"

"Of course," she said, starting her car. "You get to say when."

The last time Joe had tried to bring Chloe here yellow police tape had barred their entry.

"Do you think we'll ever move back, Dad?"

Chloe had been quiet during the drive from The Meadows. She'd been quiet a lot these past two years.

Although she'd been coming out of her shell this summer, even last night when he'd been trying to have a heart-to-heart talk following that episode at the pond, she'd been reserved. He'd assured her he'd been too far away to see her, but secretly he was still cringing at the evidence that his little girl was growing up. He'd missed so much. It wasn't only because of Noreen's disappearance, but because of his career, too. He had a lot to make up for, a lot to make right, and he was starting here, at the house he and his daughter had shared with Noreen.

"Is that what you want, Chloe, to move back here?"

He'd expected her to say something glib, but she said nothing at all, another indication that she was growing up. She went from room to room, touching throw pillows and sculptures, tapestries and light switches. Other than him and Lila, and the cleaning service he paid to dust and polish once a month, no one had been here since the police had been forced to drop the investigation due to insufficient evidence. At some point he was going to have to decide what to do with the property.

When he noticed that Chloe was staring at the family photograph on the living room wall, he laid his hand on her narrow shoulder. "It seems like so long, you know?" she whispered.

"I know."

"I thought Ramon would never take this picture. Turn your head this way, put your hand there, stand up straight, smile."

"You knew his name?" Wondering if he was reading more into her sudden fascination with the clasp on her watch, he said, "Did Ramon come to the house often?"

"Just a few times."

A photographer who made house calls? Joe barely remembered what the man looked like. He'd been from D.C., hadn't he? He wracked his brain trying to recall a last name. He wanted to ask Chloe how Noreen had acted around him, what she remembered, what she'd seen, but it wouldn't have been fair to plant doubts in his daughter's mind.

"He did a nice job that day. The photograph on the wall is beautiful, but this was my favorite pose."

They were upstairs now, and Chloe was going through her old bedroom. She opened her closet then closed it, doing the same with drawer after drawer. Finally looking at the tiny photo Joe held under her nose, she giggled. It reminded him of the way she'd giggled the day it was taken.

It wasn't long before she said, "We can go now."

"That's all you're taking?" He gestured to the lop-eared stuffed rabbit under her arm and the locket hooked over her finger.

"Nothing fits me anymore."

Wondering if she was referring to her clothes or the house itself, he went to her nightstand where a photograph of Noreen in a mother-of-pearl frame still sat. He tucked it under his arm and followed his daughter from the room.

In the foyer, he glanced back at the larger-than-life family portrait. He'd looked at it dozens of times. Staring at Noreen's image today, he noted the way the light caught in her eyes and hair. Her smile was radiant. All this time he'd thought it was theatrics. Now he wondered.

"Have you heard anything from your mother, Chloe? Anything at all?"

"No. It's like she really has disappeared off the face of the planet." She looked one more time at the photo before turning away. "If we go home now, we'll be back before Katherine brings dinner."

Had Chloe realized she'd just called The Meadows home? He decided not to point it out to her.

He was learning.

Katherine woke up doubting her ability to make rational decisions. What had she done?

She'd been spontaneous and wanton twice in the same day. Surely it was temporary insanity. Either that or it was lust. Perhaps they were the same thing.

By the time she'd swung her feet over the side of the

bed, she was rehearsing what she would say to Heath. She would inform him that last night hadn't changed what had gone wrong between them two years ago. Maybe she would plead insanity. No, she wouldn't plead, period. She would simply inform him that—oh, goodness, she lost her train of thought. Her mind went momentarily blank as she became aware of sensitive places that hadn't been sensitive in a very long time.

She told herself that their problems wouldn't disappear forever simply because they'd lost their minds in passion. All because he'd seen her naked. Goodness, he'd seen her naked over and over throughout the night. And she'd seen him.

What about the past?

What about the future?

Both questions filled her with doubts. She had to talk to him about this. Where was he, anyway?

She listened intently to the silence. His sheet was rumpled, his pillow cool to the touch, suggesting he'd been up for a while. Squinting, she peered at the clock radio.

She swooped closer, doubting her eyes. Ten o'clock? In the morning?

How could that be? She never overslept. Not even when she had the flu. Cinching the sash of her robe tight, she ran downstairs. "Heath?"

The breakfast room was empty, the table exactly

as she'd left it yesterday morning. The toaster was out in the kitchen, though, along with the jar of instant coffee. Next to those items was a note.

It's too late to take it all back, Katherine. I'll see you at dinner at The Meadows.
Heath
P.S. I'll bring pizzas—enough to feed a small army.

Even the hand she'd clasped over her mouth couldn't contain her dismay. She'd forgotten all about dinner.

It was Saturday and everybody was acting weird. It was disgusting, really. Chloe put the lop-eared rabbit on her bed then flopped down next to it only to spring back up again. She wrinkled up her nose because she smelled like the goats, but that wasn't what she found disgusting. It was the men.

A person would think they'd never seen a woman naked before. Talk about goo-goo eyes. Her dad couldn't keep his eyes off Lila. The way Heath looked at Katherine wasn't any better. Even Grandpa was acting strange. She didn't know what his problem was.

Lila had said something was in the water around here. That wasn't true, because she'd seen Rusty drink plenty of water this past week, and he didn't even know she was alive.

He was still working on his stupid car when Chloe wandered up the lane. Being careful not to appear too interested, she eased a little closer. "Dad said you've been helping clean things up around here."

"I guess."

It wasn't difficult to keep from staring into his eyes for too long because he didn't even look up. She leaned over the engine, peering into the vast void the way he was. She didn't understand what was so interesting about a bunch of hoses and wires and globs of grease.

"So how is my dad to work for?"

"He's okay, I guess."

She wished she had more experience talking to boys. The guys she had come into contact with at school-sponsored events had launched into a never-ending recital of what they liked and where they went and how much fun they had. Rusty was different. Keeping the conversation going fell to her, which wasn't good, because her mouth went dry whenever she came within twenty feet of him, and she couldn't think of anything interesting to say.

"Is Rusty a nickname?"

"What do you think?"

She thought he could have been a little nicer. "What's your real name?"

He didn't utter a sound.

"Does your name begin with an *R* like Ryan's and Ricky's?"

"Forget about it."

"What is it?"

"I'm not telling you."

Since it was too late to appear uninterested, she decided to come right out and ask for what she wanted. "If you want to keep it a secret, it's fine with me. I'd rather have a ride in your car sometime, anyway."

"It's going to take a long time to get it running. Besides, I don't have my license yet."

Just then Lila laughed. Like always, it seemed to float out of her, uncurling like mist into the atmosphere. She was talking to Chloe's dad, who was leaning on the handle of his hoe as if he had all the time in the world. Something about seeing them together made Chloe's chest hurt. It felt like another step in losing her mother completely. "Lila says she's not sleeping with my dad."

She was glad Rusty wasn't looking at her because her face felt like it was on fire.

"I wouldn't know," he said.

"It's okay. I believe her. You can't believe just anybody, you know. She's not too bad, considering. I sure don't know what possessed her to let Darci experiment with her hair, though. My mother never would have had her hair done at Darci's."

"My mother used to work there."

Oh sure, now he looked at her. Her face flamed all over again. Since all she could do at this point was salvage what was left of her dignity, she said, "Evidently Darci hasn't found anybody decent to replace your mom. How long ago did she work there?"

"What difference does it make?"

She remembered what Ryan had said about his mother leaving. Chloe had heard bad things about Bud Streeter. She couldn't imagine how awful having a father like that would be. "Do you ever think about driving away in your car and never coming back?"

Was that what her mother had done? Had she hailed a cab and never looked back? Chloe glanced across the driveway again. For a long time she'd been terrified her dad might have done something bad to her mom. Lila seemed to believe in him. That gave Chloe hope that maybe she should, too. She felt bad, though, because that meant her mom most likely left her of her own free will. Maybe she just hadn't wanted to stay. With her.

"I'd come back for my brothers," Rusty said.

Thankful to have something else to think about, she said, "That means you can take me for that ride when you get the car running."

Silence.

"Right?"

"Sure. Maybe. I guess."

Such enthusiasm. She considered kicking him in the shins but opted for a more ladylike approach.

"Where would you take me?" He was looking at the engine again so she didn't waste her time or energy trying to appear blasé. "To the movies?"

"Why would I do that?"

"Where then?" she persisted.

"How should I know? To the playground?"

She didn't care if her hands did fly to her hips or her mouth did drop open. Flicking her hair behind her shoulders, she said, "And they say the *fog* is dense in this valley."

Lila had been keeping an eye on Chloe. When the girl stomped off, Lila followed. Chloe had to veer to the left to keep from barreling into Heath on her way to the house. Before Lila could warn her, Chloe had already ducked in order to keep from getting beaned by a wild softball.

"Watch it!" the girl grumbled despite the fact that it had been her own fault.

"Heath's teachin' me 'n Ryan to play ball."

"Ryan and me," Pepper said, automatically correcting his speech from the chaise lounge on the front porch.

For several weeks now, there had been a new rhythm to Lila's days at The Meadows. The newly painted house reminded her of a softhearted old woman, her arms spread wide, a clean white apron covering her ample bosom. The debris had been cleared away throughout the yard, the lawn freshly cut. The garden plants grew more every day. The goats hadn't gotten out since Ricky had discovered the loose board in the fence and Joe had mended it. Louie the rooster still crowed long past dawn, and every day laughter rolled through the meadows, across the smooth surface of the pond, into the orchard and beyond the boundaries of her property.

Something different was in the air today. She didn't know what was going on, but there were goose bumps on her arms and a vibration beneath her feet. She couldn't shake the feeling that something was about to be settled, or perhaps revealed.

"You wanna play?" Ricky asked Chloe.

Everybody was watching now, even Rusty.

"You mean play a game?" Chloe asked. "A baseball game?"

Heath glanced at Katherine, and then he looked even harder at Joe. "That's a good idea," the mayor said as if reaching a conclusion long overdue. "Hey, everybody! Gather round. Chloe and the boys want to play some ball. What are there, ten of us? That's five to a team."

"Heath," Katherine said in a tone of voice Lila had never heard her use. "I really don't think—"

"Good. Don't think. You can be on Chloe's team. Rusty? You and Joe are team captains. Choose your players."

Lila could feel Joe's tension. He still hadn't said anything, but he wasn't taking his eyes off Heath. He'd been pensive after he and Chloe had returned from their house in Murray this morning. Joe had shown Lila the name of the photography studio stamped on the back of Noreen's photograph, and he'd mentioned that Chloe had known the man by his first name. He'd placed a call to the P.I. he hadn't heard from in months. Was that what these goose bumps were about? She couldn't tell. She only knew that there was a whisper in the sky, out of range of her hearing.

The goats stood near the fence, watching. Birds landed on the wire overhead. Even the half-wild barn cats came out of hiding. It was as if they sensed whatever Lila sensed. Whatever it was, they weren't afraid.

Joe's father said, "I've got to get back to the tavern."

"Oh, no you don't, old man," Pepper taunted. "If you leave, the teams will be uneven. Trust me, it's like riding a bike. Who's got the balls?"

"Let's keep in mind there are children present, shall we?" Katherine admonished.

"I was referring to baseballs. Geez, Katherine, what's on your mind?"

Whether they'd intended to or not, everybody had drawn closer as if being reeled in. They formed a circle around Chloe and the little boys. Some sort of battle lines had been drawn. They were calling it a ball game, but none of them were that naive. There was more than baseball at stake here, and whatever was going on, it was between Joe and Heath, between Heath and Katherine, between Pepper and Joe's dad.

"All right, everybody," Heath said, still engaged in a stare-down with Joe. "Let's play ball."

CHAPTER 15

Joe had better things to do than play baseball.

It was too damn hot. He was too stinking old. He didn't need this grief. And Heath Avery knew it.

"It's just a game," Katherine said quietly as everyone gathered around the makeshift bases.

"A friendly game for the boys," Lila added.

"You don't have to do it, son," his father told him.

Yes, he did. Heath knew that, too.

Ryan and Chloe had run to the cabin and brought back Joe's old ball gloves. It turned out that Heath still carried his old bat and ball in the trunk of his car. "Once a ballplayer, always a ballplayer," he said from the old grain sack they were using for home plate.

Joe wanted to punch him in the nose, and had for two years. They'd been rivals from the beginning, strong competitors who'd managed to be friends, too. Once.

There were no stands full of fans, no organ music, no television cameras or radio announcers. Chloe was catching, and Lila was already on first base. Not even her quiet presence could undo the knots inside him this afternoon. The women were right. This wasn't about baseball. Of all the emotions running through him, anger was the easiest to identify. If the kids hadn't been around, he would have taken great satisfaction in throwing a wild ball. As it was, he had to be content with striking the mayor out, although it would have been more satisfying if Heath would have minded.

Oblivious to the undercurrents, eight-year-old Ricky was up next. After a quick lesson from Heath, the boy assumed his position. Everyone moved closer, and Joe lobbed the ball toward the bat. Ricky swung, and Chloe yelled, "Strike one!"

Heath whispered something to the boy. This time Ricky held the bat still and Joe hit his target. Even Joe found it comical when Ricky started one way, and then the other, before following Heath's direction and racing toward first.

Pepper and Heath cheered at all the "mishaps" that allowed Ricky to reach the base safely. Rusty took his turn at bat. A little while ago Joe had noticed the way he'd watched Chloe flounce away. It wasn't the first time he'd caught that fleeting look in the boy's eyes. It was unfortunate for Rusty that Joe remembered how it felt to be fifteen. He thought about how fast Chloe was growing up, and how one strategically placed baseball would keep his daughter's virtue safe for a month. Another part of Joe wanted to give the boy a pitch he could smack across the road.

But Rusty didn't immediately assume the proper batting position. Instead, he faced Joe. A stare-down ensued. The kid wanted his pitch straight and real. No tricks. No favors. Just honesty.

Joe wound up, and released a ball that dropped a foot as it crossed the plate. Rusty swung and missed. Now that he knew what he was dealing with, he gripped the bat tighter and bent his knees a little more. The next pitch was outside, but he made contact with the third ball, smacking it straight and hard.

Joe put his glove in front of his face out of self defense. And caught the ball.

"Holy sh—I mean, you're out!" Chloe called.

Rusty looked surprised, but not humiliated or cocky. Joe removed his ball glove and shook his stinging hand.

The ball game progressed haphazardly after that. Lila and Ricky scored. Pepper struck out and broke a nail in the process. She asked Joe's father if he wanted to kiss it and make it better. When she fell over in left field in the next inning, she asked him again.

The next time the opposition was up to bat, Joe turned his attention to Katherine. He doubted it was a coincidence that she and Heath were on opposite teams today. Katherine was giving Heath the cold shoulder. So what else was new? For once, Heath wasn't placating her. Normally, Joe would have put his money on Katherine. Today, he was glad he wasn't a betting man.

Katherine didn't know what possessed her to agree to this game. Yes, she did. Chloe had pleaded, and she hadn't been able to say no. Now, here she was, a forty-year-old woman in street shoes rounding third base, of all things. Directly ahead of her, Heath was defending home. Was there no rest for the weary? No justice?

She slowed as she neared, looking for a clear path around him. "You're in my way," she said tightly.

"What are you going to do about it?"

She felt everyone looking at them. "Is it fair to block the baseline?" she yelled to Joe.

"Leave Joe out of this," Heath said ominously. "You want to talk about last night? Last year? Two years ago? Ten? Fine, let's talk."

"This is neither the time nor the place."

"This is the perfect place. And there's no time like the present."

"Heath, please."

"Please, what? We've done this your way for two years. And where has it gotten us? I'm not going to roll over and play dead anymore, Katherine. Throw me the damn ball, Rusty, so I can tag her out."

Joe was approaching.

"Stay out of this, McCaffrey."

"Don't yell at Joe. None of this is his fault. And get out of my way, Heath. You're goaltending."

Chloe's eyes were huge. But Ryan and Ricky were backing up as if they thought the confrontation would blow up in their faces. "It's all right, boys," Heath said, barely taking his eyes off his wife. "I won't hurt her." His throat convulsed and his voice dropped in volume. "I never wanted to hurt you, Katherine."

She tried to go around him, first one way and then the other. He ignored her every command.

"Bring it on, honey," he said. "There's only one way, and that's over the top."

Whatever had caused her to shed her clothes at the pond last night reared again. She barreled into him, sending them both sailing backward. He landed with a quiet "Oomph" in the soft grass, his arms going around her, cushioning her fall.

"I hope you're happy!" she said, her face inches from his.

He rolled her underneath him, pressing evidence of just how happy he was becoming against her.

"There are children present," she whispered.

"Hold still and give me a minute."

Lila went to stand beside Joe. Even the birds on the wires overhead and the goats in the fenced pasture were losing interest in Heath and Katherine. Pepper was flirting outrageously with Joe's dad. Chloe was talking to Rusty, and Ryan and Ricky were lying on their backs, staring up at the sky. Perhaps because everyone else had their own agendas, no one seemed concerned with Katherine's dilemma except Katherine and Heath.

Life was like that, Lila thought to herself. Sensationalism wore off eventually. Look at her situation. And look at Joe's. It couldn't have been easy for him to pick up that baseball today. And yet he'd done it.

"Are you okay?" she asked Joe.

He looked her in the eye. "My shoulder's on fire and my arm isn't much better, but you know something, Lila? I'm going to be all right. What about you?"

Earlier she'd told him about the gut instinct she'd awakened with this morning. She didn't know what it meant, but she couldn't shake the feeling that something was about to be made known to them all. She wasn't having a vision. Nothing was written in the clouds. It wasn't anything concrete. But it was something, something unexplainable and otherworldly, and it made her sit up and take notice and it gave her the conviction to pay attention to what was about to happen. Joe accepted that part of her. He believed in that part of her, the way she believed in him.

Heath's cell phone rang while he and Katherine were untangling arms and legs and tempers. He tossed the ball to Joe. Motioning for them to continue the game without him, he moved out of hearing range to take the call.

Rusty assumed Heath's position, and the game continued. Ryan's swing came out of the blue. He was a natural and he scored a grand slam home run. A passerby would have thought they were all on the same team, the way everybody cheered.

Lila continued to watch Heath. When he closed the phone, ran a hand through his hair and looked at her, she felt an ominous foreboding.

"I hate to break this up," he said. The seriousness in his voice had even the little boys taking notice.

"Who was it?" Katherine asked.

"That was the sheriff from Shenandoah County. Two hikers discovered something in a cave up there."

"What did they discover?" Joe's father was the only one present with the ability to speak.

"They found a woman's body."

Chloe screamed, already starting to run. Joe caught her, held her.

"They think it's my mother, don't they?" she cried.

"They can't possibly know that, Chloe. We'll find out. Together."

Church bells pealed in the distance, proof that it was finally morning. The back door creaked when Joe entered. He never had mastered opening it sound-lessly the way Lila could. She was waiting for him in the kitchen with a pot of fresh coffee and a sleepy "Good morning."

He helped himself to coffee, but didn't immediately drink it.

"Is Chloe still asleep?" she asked, removing a piece of straw from his hair.

Heath and Katherine had taken Rusty, Ryan and Ricky home to their trailer over on Waterwheel Road after supper last night. Pepper had gone to McCaffrey's, only to return early, agitated and uneasy. The discovery of a body in a cave was the talk of the town.

Poor Chloe had been inconsolable. At one point she'd taken a walk out to the barn, only to race back to the house, hysterical because the goat was in trouble. While Joe tried to locate a veterinarian who made house calls that time of night, Lila and Chloe had hurried to the barn.

By the time Joe joined them, Curly was calm and in full-blown labor. The goat may have been an older mother, but she knew exactly what to do. Lila, Joe and Chloe kept vigil until the kid came. It was the first birth Lila had ever witnessed. Chloe, too.

Sitting in the fragrant straw in that warm barn, fog swirling across the crescent moon in the otherwise dark sky, Joe told Chloe about the day she was born, how he'd raced to get there in time, how beautiful she'd been, and how strong she still was. Chloe had fallen asleep listening. Unwilling to wake her, but unwilling to leave her, too, he'd hunkered down in the straw with her. Now that the long night was finally over, he leaned against the counter, crossed his ankles and looked at Lila.

"What?" she whispered.

"Chloe's waking up. She wanted a few minutes alone with Curly and the new baby. I'm glad Myrtle Ann brought you here."

She walked straight into his arms. When Chloe came inside, she stepped aside so Chloe could absorb her father's comfort.

Pepper got up eventually. Breakfast was eaten, showers taken, and minutes counted. They left the television and radio off, and the phone plugged in.

They all heard the car pull into the driveway. Heath and Katherine got out, and came in together.

"There has been some news," Katherine said.

When her voice trailed away and she couldn't continue, Heath took over. "There were two people in that cave. A woman and a man."

"Noreen?" Joe asked, squeezing Chloe's hand.

"This woman has been there longer than two years," Heath answered.

"Then she can't be my mother!" Chloe exclaimed,

jumping up and down. "That means my mom probably isn't dead."

"How long has this woman been there?" Lila asked, rubbing the goose bumps on her arms.

"A long time. They think it's Brenda Streeter."

Chloe buried her face in Joe's shirt.

Joe and Heath looked at one another over the tops of the women's heads. "Do they know who's responsible for putting her there?" Joe asked.

"They're looking for Bud."

"Where are the boys?" Joe asked. "Has anybody told them?"

"I'm going there now."

"Wait, Heath," Joe said, "I'll go with you."

Pepper was late for work on Sunday.

She'd waited for Joe and Heath to return to The Meadows after breaking the news to the kids. They'd brought the boys with them. It seemed their father hadn't gone home last night. The police had an APB out for Bud's arrest.

Of course he'd done it. Why else would he have slunk away like the sniveling coward he was at the first inkling that a body had been discovered in a cave? The answer sickened Pepper. What kind of a monster was capable of murdering two people and then laughing about it in his beer for seven years? That answer sickened her, too.

She parked in the back alley beside Joseph's car.

She was surprised to find that the back door was locked. Yawning—what a horrible night it had been—she strolled around to the front of the building. Rebellion Street was practically deserted. Where was everyone? It seemed everything was slightly off-kilter this afternoon.

"The back door's still locked, Joseph. Are you trying to tell me something?" she called after entering through the front door.

The main room of the bar was empty, and eerily quiet. It was Sunday, after all. Still, she was relieved when she heard sounds coming from the storeroom.

"What did you drop?" She went directly to the back room. Wishing her eyes would adjust to the dimness, she said, "Why are you working in the dark?"

By the time her vision cleared, it was too late. Joseph was lying on the floor in a pool of liquid, shards of glass all around him. And Bud Streeter had stepped between her and the door.

CHAPTER 16

"Move. Damn it, I said move!"

Pepper smelled whiskey and tasted fear, but there was nothing wrong with her hearing. It was her feet that weren't fully operational.

The cold, hard object Bud Streeter shoved into her ribs penetrated her panic. She managed to put one foot in front of the other. Joseph still hadn't moved.

Oh God oh God oh God.

"It's his own fault," Bud sputtered, pushing her toward the door. "All he had to do was open the till, but no, he wanted to be a hero."

Pepper glanced at Bud's pitted face. Murder? Revenge? He looked capable of anything.

Oh God oh God oh God.

Radcliffe hadn't prepared her for this. Life hadn't prepared her for this. She heard one of her sister's favorite old taunts. *Ready or not.* A sob lodged sideways in her throat. She wanted to see Emily again, and Gwen, and her parents and her grandfather. And Lila and Katherine. And Joseph McCaffrey the *first*.

What had Bud done?

"You're going to go out there and open the till. Nice and slow." He motioned with the gun.

Oh, God, it really was a gun. Her heart continued to race. This happened to other people. Not her.

Was there any way out of this? There had to be. Think. Think. "If I give you the money, you'll let me go?"

"Wouldn't have thought an educated rich girl like you would be paranoid."

"Paranoid is when you think the man in front of you is following you." For God's sake, why didn't she just shoot herself?

But he wasn't offended. In fact, he laughed, and she thought maybe, just maybe, if she kept him talking, he wouldn't kill her.

"I like a woman with a sense of humor. I planned to leave you in the storeroom with Pops, but I think maybe you and me ought'a take a little ride."

He ran the barrel of his pistol up her bare arm, raising goose bumps, and bile. And she knew that if she left this tavern with him, someday some hikers would discover *her* body in a cave.

"Everybody thinks you've headed for the hills. I'm surprised you're still in Murray."

"Be a good girl and shut the hell up. Damn women anyway, always running at the mouth. I finally figured out who you remind me of. Ever heard of Mad Ann Bailey? She lived 'round here a few hundred years ago. Native Americans killed her husband, so she started dressing in men's clothes. They say she was a tall beauty who carried an ax, a rifle and a tomahawk. Spent the rest of her life avenging her husband's death. Became a legend in these parts, so you see? Murder ain't always wrong. Sometimes it's justified. Sometimes it even goes down in history."

Pepper didn't know if he was insane or if the thought of going to prison was pushing him closer to the edge. She had to keep him talking until she could think of something constructive to do. But what did one say to a man like him?

"Was *Brenda's* death justified?"

"She and Bruce Stavinski thought they were pullin' one over on me. They played me for a fool. Guess we know who the fools were, though, don't we? She was a worthless whore."

She was the mother of his children, but Pepper wasn't about to incense him by defending her. "Do you think Noreen McCaffrey is dead, too?"

"Joe might be a big shot, but he didn't deserve a whore like her, either."

"Do you think Joe killed her?"

"If he did, he's a bigger man than I thought. It takes guts."

He shoved her toward the bar with so much force she stumbled. They'd taken the long way, stopping to lock the front door. Now nobody would be able to get in to help her.

"Open it."

Her fingers shook as she opened the till. Now that he had access to the money, he would kill her. Or worse.

"Take the money out," he commanded.

"Have at it," she answered. "I need a drink."

She left him staring at the cash while she reached for a bottle of whiskey and a glass. He must have been feeling confident, because he eyed the bottle and licked his lips. "Make mine a double."

"Take a load off," she said.

He wasn't that gullible and she wasn't that lucky. "I'm comfortable right here." He waved the gun in her direction, watching her closely, as if he expected her to throw the liquor in his face. The thought had crossed her mind, but since death was only a squeeze of a trigger away, she handed the glass to him then poured one for herself.

"Cheers," she said, taking a sip.

She caught him looking at her mouth. It was now or never. Taking another sip, she wet her lips to keep his eyes from drifting while she reached blindly for the bottle. She swung it at his head with so much force her hand buzzed and the bottle shattered on impact. He stumbled toward her and struck her before taking aim.

A man came flying over the bar yelling for her to get down. There was an explosion of sound and of pain. She landed hard, and closed her eyes, something warm soaking into her von Furstenberg silk blouse.

If Pepper was in heaven, heaven was very noisy.

She heard voices and echoes and sirens. She thought she was being lifted. But she could have been dreaming.

By the time she managed to pry her eyes open, she was on a gurney. A man in a white coat was listening to her heart and a woman was starting an IV. The police were here, too. There was so much movement it made her dizzy.

"Joseph, is that you?" It wasn't easy to see past the white coats.

Joseph leaned close and swallowed hard. "Were you expecting somebody else?"

The EMTs stepped aside.

"You're not dead?" she asked.

He shook his head. His right eye was swollen shut and there were cuts on his hands and his face.

"Am I?" she whispered.

"Thank God, no."

That explained the searing pain in her side. Her eyes

tried their darnedest to close, but she fought it with everything she had. "Joseph?" she whispered again.

"Yes?"

"You don't pay me enough to put up with this."

He rested his forehead on her shoulder a moment. When he lifted his face, his eyes were wet. "You really should think about quitting."

"Quit? I'm going to need a raise."

Not so much as a breeze stirred the air at The Meadows. Bud Streeter was in the county jail and Pepper was in the hospital. She'd lost some blood, but the bullet had missed major organs and arteries. She was going to fully recover. Lila wasn't so sure about Joe's father, although most of his injuries were emotional, not physical. She knew from experience that those often took longer to heal.

According to Joe Sr., Pepper had smashed a bottle of Jack Daniel's over Bud Streeter's head as he pulled the trigger. Leave it to Pepper to keep her head during a crisis. Joe Sr. had gone flying over the bar, knocking the gun out of Bud's hand before he could squeeze off another round. Between the two of them, they'd saved Pepper's life and captured Bud in the process.

Katherine and Heath had arrived at The Meadows shortly after Lila, Joe and Chloe returned from the hospital. They'd brought Ryan, Ricky and Rusty with them. Lila could only imagine how those kids felt. All these years they'd been told their mother had deserted them, when in reality she'd been dead, murdered by their father. The younger two looked to Rusty for guidance. He was only fifteen. How could he handle this and them? All three were being made wards of the court, and were staying here until someone from the county came for them.

Chloe had tried to draw them into conversation. She'd even tried to coax Ryan and Ricky to climb her favorite apple tree with her. They hadn't, though. They were sticking close to Rusty.

"Why do bad things like this happen?" Chloe implored. "What have they done to deserve this?"

Katherine was at the stove, cooking enough food to feed twenty people. She turned around, such innate sadness in her eyes. "They didn't do anything to deserve this. These things happen, but not as punishment."

"When I thought it was my mother in that cave, I felt like there was a brick inside my chest. That's how they feel, isn't it?"

"They'll get through this, Chloe," Lila said.

Chloe turned puffy eyes to Lila. "You knew it wasn't my mother in that cave, didn't you?"

Lila sat down at the table and took Chloe's hand in hers. "I hoped it wasn't. The only thing I knew for sure was that if it was, your father couldn't have done it."

Joe and Heath wandered inside looking miserable and helpless. Through the window, Lila could see the boys. The hood was up on Rusty's car, but all three of them were sitting together on the ground in the shade, their arms resting on their bent knees, their backs against the side of Myrtle Ann's old Corvair.

Chloe picked at her fingernails. She fidgeted. She jiggled her foot. There was something about the covert glance she cast Heath that caused Lila to say, "What is it, Chloe?"

She looked at Heath again, and this time she didn't look away. "I know something. Something bad."

"What is it?" Lila asked again.

"I don't know if I should tell anybody."

"You can say it, Chloe," Heath said.

"I saw you at our house that day," she whispered. "I heard you and Daddy yelling."

Tears coursed down Katherine's cheeks as Heath said, "I didn't know you were home."

Chloe sniffled. "I was supposed to stay in my room. Mom always told me not to snoop. She said it would get me in trouble someday." She turned to her father. "I knew how mad you were, Daddy. I thought maybe you were mad enough, you know?"

"I could never be that angry, Chloe."

He opened his arms, and she went into them. "I know that now. Lila always knew it, but I was so scared. I mean, if you'd done it, I'd be like Rusty and his brothers. I'd be a ward of the county. It's why I took the home pregnancy kit and threw it away. I was afraid it might not be your baby."

The room, all of a sudden, was perfectly quiet.

Joe stood close enough that Lila could feel the tension in him. "What home pregnancy kit?" he asked.

Chloe's eyes darted nervously between her father and Heath. "The one in the waste basket in her bathroom."

"Are you sure it wasn't something else?"

"It turned blue, Dad."

"Your mother was pregnant?" he asked.

Lila recalled when Joe had told her that he and Noreen hadn't been intimate for months prior to her disappearance. If it wasn't Joe's baby, whose?

One by one, everyone looked at Heath.

Katherine couldn't believe it had come to this. For two years she'd done everything in her power to put this out of her mind. And now, here it was, up to her. "If Noreen was pregnant," she said, "it wasn't with Heath's child."

He reached for her hand, held it. He'd always been a proud man, so it couldn't have been easy for him to turn to Joe and say, "It's true. Even if we had gone through with the unthinkable, it wouldn't have been my baby. I can't father a child, any child. It's the reason

Katherine and I don't have children. I never should have been at your house in the first place that day, but my ego had taken a beating, a paltry excuse, isn't it?"

Katherine saw her husband look at Chloe, and knew he was leaving a great deal unsaid. She and Heath hadn't broached this subject in two years, but what he'd told Joe was true. She didn't condone the fact that Joe had found Heath in his bedroom, kissing Noreen. She wasn't sure she could ever forgive it. But she understood it.

What had gone wrong between them had started years before Noreen disappeared. Katherine had always been able to make her dreams come true. No matter what it took, when she set her sights on something, she didn't give up. Heath had wanted to give her everything her heart desired. All her life she'd known she would become a mother. Charts and doctors' appointments and seeing her disappointment month after month had de-manned him. She'd wanted a child so badly, for years it had taken over everything in her life. Discovering he was the reason there would be no children had been the last straw for him.

Did that give him the right to kiss his best friend's wife, or to allow her to kiss him? To this day, the thought of it turned Katherine's stomach. She'd always wondered what would have happened if Joe hadn't walked in on them that day. She hadn't known about it at the time. She only knew that Heath and Joe had had a falling out. Later, she'd heard about the argument between Joe and Noreen. After Noreen disappeared, Katherine had put it all together. One night, she'd confronted Heath, and he hadn't been able to deny it.

Heath was looking around as if deciding what to say in front of an audience. When his eyes met hers, it was as if they were alone in the room. "I didn't have an affair. As God is my witness, it's the truth. I wish I could say with absolute certainty that I would have been man enough to stop even if Joe hadn't come home when he did. But the way we've been living these past two years isn't living, Katherine. After the other night, I can't go back to the way we were."

She'd known that yesterday when he'd refused to let her pass him during that ball game. She didn't want to go back to the way they'd been, but she didn't know if she could move forward, either. "I don't know what to do," she whispered.

He reached for her other hand. "There are three boys outside who need a family. I've seen the way you are with them. You've been mothering them for weeks. Just because I can't father children doesn't mean we can't be parents."

"Cool!" Chloe exclaimed.

For once, Katherine ignored Chloe and concentrated all her energy on her husband. She loved those kids and he knew it. "You're fighting dirty."

One corner of his mouth lifted just enough to hint that the worst was behind them. "I'll fight any way I have to for the love of one incredible woman. Come on, Katherine. What do you say?"

Their marriage needed work. How on earth could he even suggest taking this on right now?

"Three boys?" she whispered. "All at once? I've always pictured myself with daughters."

"Are you going to let that stop you?" he asked.

Katherine's back straightened, and her chin came up. She wasn't going to let anything stop her. "We need to talk about this. We need to talk about our marriage. We need time."

"The social worker will be here soon. Ryan, Rusty and Ricky are running out of time. What do you want to do?"

She looked at him, then around the room, and finally out the window. All at once she knew without a doubt what she wanted. "We need to talk to the boys. And we need to do it soon."

He swung her around right there in Lila's kitchen.

"For heaven's sake, Heath, put me down this instant." When her feet touched the floor again, she let him take her hand. Together, they went outside.

Lila, Joe and Chloe watched from the window.

Ricky jumped up as soon as Heath and Katherine started talking. Ryan rose a little more slowly. Rusty got up and walked the other way.

"Uh-oh," Chloe said. "That's not a good sign."

Katherine went after him, but he shook off the gentle hand she placed on his arm. Heath said something to him, and Rusty turned around defiantly.

"What do you think Heath's saying?" Chloe asked.

Lila answered without taking her eyes off the scene unfolding outdoors. "He's offering Rusty a home for him and his brothers in exchange for a family."

Katherine was right, Lila thought. Heath did fight dirty, for Rusty might have been able to refuse for himself, but he would do what was best for his brothers.

"I think Rusty's thinking about it," Chloe said.

"It'll require a great deal of paperwork and patience, but Heath is giving Rusty his word."

"How do you know?" Chloe asked.

"Just look at them. What else could it mean when a man holds out his hand to a fifteen-year-old boy?"

They all knew what it meant when the boy accepted that handshake. They were all witnessing the birth of a family.

Katherine went to Heath and Rusty, Ryan on one side of her, Ricky on the other. She was crying as she hugged them each in turn.

"Wow," Chloe said. "Pepper got shot. Grandpa's a

hero. Bud Streeter's in jail. Heath and Katherine are getting three kids. And Ricky, Ryan and Rusty are getting new parents."

"A busy day," Joe agreed.

"Wait until I tell my friends at school."

Joe didn't say anything to Chloe yet, but he wasn't planning to send her back to boarding school. He wasn't sure how he would approach the subject, but she'd spent too many years growing up without him. They needed to be a family before it was too late. His daughter needed it, and so did he.

Katherine and Heath and the kids came in. Lila and Chloe set the table while Katherine insisted the boys wash their hands. Her bossiness made everything feel almost normal. They all sat down together in their usual places, Heath on one end of the table, Joe as far away as he could get. At the last minute Joe picked up his plate and moved to Pepper's usual place opposite Heath. It was extremely symbolic. His wince, however, was real.

"Is that shoulder sore?" Katherine asked.

"Everything's sore." Joe held up his hand, showing Rusty the bruise.

The boy's grin was symbolic, too.

The social worker arrived before they'd finished eating. Heath made the introductions, saying simply, "I'd like you to meet my family."

"It looks like everyone's here," the social worker said.

"Not quite everybody," Chloe said.

Joe expected her to mention that her mother was missing.

Instead, she said, "Have you ever seen a day-old goat?"

"I can't say that I have." Before the woman left, she was on a first-name basis with all the goats, including the newest one, Billy.

The mountain of paperwork had been started. Thanks to Heath's status as the mayor of Murray, Judge Matthews was allowing the boys to go home with Heath and Katherine. First thing Monday morning it would become official and the long process would be underway.

After Heath and Katherine and the Streeter brothers left, Chloe wandered outside to check on the newest addition to The Meadows. Lila drove back to the hospital to see Pepper.

Joe took the rowboat out, lost in thought. The sinking yellow sun turned the mountaintops orange and backlit the willow trees lining the long gravel driveway. The house was painted, the meadows cleared, the garden growing. His work here was done.

His cell phone rang before he had time to think about that.

He put it to his ear and listened. He clenched his

jaw, the words in his ear simple and direct. "You're sure it was her?" he asked.

The private investigator relayed the information he'd uncovered since their last conversation yesterday. He'd found Noreen. All this time, Joe thought, the clue to her whereabouts had been staring him in the face. The photographer who'd taken that family portrait had left the country the same time Noreen disappeared. Unlike Noreen, he'd left a forwarding address.

"As soon as you've verified their whereabouts, let me know." Joe looked toward the big house, the orchard and the barns. A busy day, he'd told Chloe a while ago. The day wasn't over yet.

CHAPTER 17

Pepper knew without opening her eyes that she wasn't alone in her hospital room. How could she have known that unless what Lila said was true?

All women became slightly psychic eventually.

Mercy, apparently even her.

Her family had arrived yesterday while she'd been in surgery. The anesthetic made it all seem like a blur. Her parents and sisters had gone out for a bite to eat a little while ago. It had been good to see them again, especially since they all apologized profusely for the part they'd played in her recent financial difficulties. Pepper wouldn't have been Pepper if she'd let them off the hook immediately. Although she could have done quite nicely without the hole in her side, she wasn't sorry about the way this situation had turned out.

Lila had visited, too. She'd perched on the side of the bed and brought Pepper up to date on everything that had happened. All these weeks they'd wondered what was between Joe and Katherine, when in reality, it had been Heath and Noreen who'd almost had an affair. Poor Katherine. Or maybe Katherine wasn't poor at all. Maybe it was all the divine unfolding of that master plan Lila was always talking about. Regardless, now Katherine and Heath had the family they'd always wanted.

"What time is it?" she asked the man watching the sun go down outside her window.

"Time for you to come home." Winston Bartholomew finally turned around.

She would have preferred to have gotten a good night's sleep before facing her grandfather. She wasn't surprised he was pressing his advantage.

"Emily wants me to come to New York to live with her. Gwen offered me their guesthouse in the Hamptons for as long as I need it. Mother's upset with you, by the way. With Dad, too. It's the first time I've ever heard her tell him I told you so out loud."

"We'll never hear the end of it, but you're going to recover and that's the most important thing. We all got a little carried away about proving our points, including you, Penelope. When you're strong enough, I have a corner office waiting for you."

"Give it to Gwen, Grandfather."

His eyes narrowed, accentuating a craggy face and a compact though still fit body. "You don't belong here."

"I'm being released the day after tomorrow."

"Don't be obtuse. You're a Bartholomew."

"Do you expect me to be relieved?"

"I expect you to—"

"Do as you say?"

That was exactly what he'd almost said. "You're above this lifestyle."

"You're a snob."

She and her grandfather had been butting heads since she'd turned thirteen. They were worse than Lila's goats. "Do we have any skeletons in our closets, Grandfather? Any Mad Ann Baileys or Lila Delaneys or J.J. McCaffreys?"

"Of course not. Do you need me to call the nurse?"

"I'm not delirious. Every family has skeletons."

"Not ours."

"Pity."

"Don't get mouthy, young lady."

"I'm almost forty years old."

He stared at her as if this was a shock. "Bartholomews don't wait tables. They don't tend bar or chase goats or go skinny-dipping and they certainly don't suffer gunshot wounds."

"Do you have a GPS lock on me or have you been having me followed?" On the heels of that thought was another. "Oh, my God. That's it! I'm the skeleton in our family closet. I'm the Mad Ann Bailey of the Bartholomew clan. I'm the woman future generations will talk about behind their hands. I'm the gypsy around the fire, Lady Godiva on the white horse. I'm Mrs. Robinson in reverse. What a relief. Thank you, Grandfather, for clearing that up for me."

She recognized the pained look that crossed his features, for she'd seen the same look often on Joseph's face. "Would you do me a favor?" she asked sweetly. "Would you ask Joseph to come in?"

Winston Bartholomew the *third* wasn't accustomed to being dismissed any more than Joseph McCaffrey the *first* was accustomed to being summoned. If Pepper was good at one thing, it was working every angle to her advantage. She wasn't born a Bartholomew for nothing.

Joseph entered furtively.

"About that raise." She rather enjoyed watching his hackles rise. "Don't even attempt to give me the 'young lady' speech. I just heard it, and it wasn't well received. Are those flowers for me?"

He looked at the bouquet he was mutilating as if wondering how it had gotten in his hand. There was something endearing about the way he offered the flowers to her.

"It wasn't your fault, Joseph. It was Bud's doing, not yours."

"I was with Penny when she died," he blurted.

Pepper wasn't accustomed to speaking about people who'd died. It was one of those subjects she'd always avoided because she never knew what to say. Today, she didn't say anything. Moving carefully, she laid the flowers on the bedside tray and waited for him to continue.

"We didn't have a lot of warning, just three weeks from the diagnosis to the end. She was so young, and I wasn't ready to say goodbye. I swore I would never go through that again."

The stubble of his beard gave him a rugged look, the bruise on his forehead was wicked, the stitches near his ear even worse. "If it's any consolation," she said quietly, "When I saw you lying on the floor in the storeroom, I thought the worst." She swallowed. "And then, when you came sliding across the bar, I could hardly believe it. I thought you moved pretty fast for—"

"An old man?"

"I was going to say you moved pretty fast for a dead man. Now that you've told me about losing your wife that sounds unfeeling. What do you see happening between us?"

He sat on the side of her bed. "If you must know, I always said that if I ever met a woman I would consider marrying I would insist she sign a prenup. Now that you took a bullet in my bar that sounds unfeeling."

She just loved a man who could give as good as he got. "You have a lot of money, do you?" she asked, tongue in cheek.

His silence drew her gaze.

"Do you?" she whispered.

He shrugged. "Over the years, I saved some money."

He probably considered a few hundred thousand a lot of money. How sweet.

"Years ago I gambled and bought Intel at six."

"You own stock in Intel?"

"Not anymore," he said.

The pain meds were making Pepper groggy. "Don't feel bad. A lot of people lost their fortunes a few years ago when the market fell."

"I sold before the market went to hell. I have a nice little retirement fund."

"How nice? How little, if you don't mind my asking. More than a cool million?"

"Oh, yes, more than that."

A medicine cart rattled past her door, and somebody's shoe squeaked. Her mind began to drift. Before she went to sleep, she had to ask one more question. "How did you know when to sell?"

He considered the question for a moment, and answered on a shrug. "I had a hunch."

A hunch. Goodness, women weren't the only ones who were a little psychic.

He placed a hand on either side of her. Hunkering closer, he said, "This age difference won't be easy to ignore. Ten years would be one thing, but twenty-one is substantial. You realize that when you're fifty-seven, I'll be seventy-eight."

She didn't tell him that when he was seventy-eight, she could very well be dead. Once a pessimist, always a pessimist. "Joseph?" she asked instead. "What are you going to do?"

"I've been thinking about selling McCaffrey's. I've always wanted to see Paris."

Paris? He truly was a man after her own heart.

"What are you going to do right now, because I was thinking that maybe you could kiss me."

"I think that could be arranged."

CHAPTER 18

The oaks and willows lining the driveway of The Meadows looked almost human in the beam of Joe's headlights. Beyond them, the light spilling from Lila's windows beckoned. He wanted to stop, to steal just a moment or two with her and soak up whatever it was that emanated from her. He didn't stop, of course. He couldn't. Not yet.

He'd just come from McCaffrey's, where he'd met with Jim Spencer, the P.I. he'd hired to find Noreen. He'd called Lila's cell phone a few minutes ago. She'd told him Chloe was online with her friends in the cabin. Lila had to be burning with curiosity, and yet she'd asked only one question. "Are you okay, Joe?"

Finding the manila envelope with his spare hand, he'd said, "I'm fine. I have to talk to Chloe. I'd like to come up to the big house later if you're still awake."

"I'm a night owl again these days. I'm sure I'll be awake."

She'd laughed, and the sound of it stayed with him

as he made his way to the end of the lane. Tucking the envelope under his arm, he went inside.

It was even darker in the cabin than it had been outside. By now he knew that didn't necessarily mean Chloe wasn't awake. She was nocturnal, too. Unlike Lila, she almost never turned on lights, preferring to roam about in the dark. He hadn't known that until this summer.

He switched on a lamp and called her name.

"Back here, Dad."

He found her in her bedroom, her face illuminated in the glow of her laptop. "I have news," he said, turning on another lamp. "It's about your mother."

She set the laptop away from her, easing from the middle of her bed until her feel dangled over the side. Her freckles were faint in this light, her hair long and straight down her back, her favorite stuffed animal on her lap. "What about her?"

"She's living in Puerto Vallarta, Mexico, Chloe."

Wonder lit her face for an instant. Just as quickly, it was snuffed out. "So she really is alive."

In her place, he would have asked if Noreen had a brain tumor or amnesia or was being held prisoner. But his daughter didn't grasp at those straws. It was as if she'd always known it would come to something more difficult to understand.

Joe handed her the black-and-whites the P.I. had

given him. While she studied the photos of Noreen that had been taken earlier today, he turned on another lamp then lowered to the bed beside her.

"She looks exactly the same," she whispered.

He knew how it felt to lose a mother. He didn't know how it felt to be abandoned by one. He wished there was some way to make this easier for her.

"She's been there all this time?" she asked. "Happy?"

He shrugged. "We don't have all the details yet."

"Does she know you found her?"

"Not yet. It's okay to cry, Chloe."

"I don't want to cry. I wish she really was dead."

Maybe she wished that now. Although he doubted the sentiment would last forever, he didn't tell her she shouldn't say it or feel it. There was nothing wrong with honesty. On the road with the team Joe had seen things that had turned his stomach. He'd been propositioned and booed, followed and cursed, but he'd never felt such disgust for anyone.

"What has she been doing? In Mexico, I mean?" she asked.

"According to her neighbors, she's been living there for two years." He didn't tell Chloe that Noreen had taken up residence in a big, rambling house overlooking the city, or that she and her new "husband" had a small son and servants at their beck and call. Tonight, Chloe only needed to know that her mother was alive.

"What are you going to do?" she asked.

It occurred to him that his little girl knew him very well. She had a strong woman's intuition for someone so young. "I'm going to get a divorce, Chloe."

He already had his attorney drawing up the papers. "My attorney and I are flying to Mexico first thing in the morning. I know you wanted me to wait the last time, but I think you and I both need me to get this over with."

"You're coming back, right?"

She was really asking if he would desert her, too. "I'll be back the day after tomorrow. Sooner if I can catch a flight out of Mexico tomorrow night. I'll call you, and you can call me as often as you want to or need to. Grandpa said you can stay with him until I get back, or, if you'd rather, I'm sure Katherine and Heath would be happy to have you stay with them for a day or two."

"Can I stay here?" she asked very softly.

"In this cabin?" he asked, ready to tell her no.

"Here at The Meadows. I need to feed the baby goat. Curly doesn't have enough milk for him. Did you know that?"

"I didn't know that, no. I'll ask Lila if she'd mind," he said.

"She won't mind."

She sighed, and he wondered when the dam would

break and her tears would start. "Do you want me to tell your mother anything when I see her?"

She started to speak, but stopped.

"What was that?" he asked, nudging her. "Unlike you women, I can't read minds."

She almost smiled then buried her face in his shoulder, her brief flirtation with shyness. "Do you think she's missed me at all?"

He thought Noreen didn't deserve such a daughter, and never had. "How could she not miss you?"

When she rolled her eyes he drew her into a hug. "I love you, Chloe."

"How could you not?" she asked.

It was his turn to almost smile.

Lila's favorite movie was on in the living room. She left it playing, the volume turned low, and wandered outside to the back porch.

She'd almost lost her best friend yesterday. She'd never been one to take people for granted, and yet today she was filled with gratitude and relief. Pepper's close call reminded her how precarious life was and how precarious those sharing it with her. She'd called her mother, and she and Chloe had visited Pepper in the hospital, and stopped over to see how Katherine and the boys were doing. Although Lila felt she was in the place she was meant to be, doing what she was meant to do, she sensed change in the air.

Since she always thought best beneath the open sky, she lowered to the top step. She hadn't turned on the porch light, and a thick layer of clouds formed a dome between her and the stars, bringing the sky close enough to touch.

Night insects competed with each other in the grass and trees. Somewhere an owl hooted. Listening for the answering call, she brought her eyes from the sky, staring into the darkness.

"You really are psychic, aren't you?" Joe's voice was deep, and came from the exact place she was looking.

Although Lila still couldn't see him, she smiled. "How long have you been waiting?"

"I just got here."

She'd never met a man who could move without making a sound. "Is Chloe all right?" she asked.

"I think she's going to be." He walked just close enough so she could make out the shape of him in the shadows. The long day showed in his posture and in the deep breath he took. "Chloe's favorite subject in school is history. She told me that a little while ago. Do you know I didn't know that? I left too much of her care to Noreen and her teachers. Until tonight, I never saw it, just like I never saw the clue to Noreen's whereabouts."

"Maybe you weren't supposed to see it until now."

"If I'd known, Pepper wouldn't have almost gotten killed yesterday."

"She wouldn't have fallen in love with your father, either," Lila said. "And Katherine and Heath might never have found their way back to each other. And Rusty, Ryan and Ricky wouldn't have a new family. And you wouldn't have gotten to know Chloe."

Fireflies flickered near the driveway. Lila held her breath, for she felt their electricity.

"You're telling me I should shut up and count my blessings?"

Lila rolled her eyes because even good men could be dense. Not that she blamed him if he was feeling overwhelmed. Discovering that Noreen had ruined him so callously and purposefully wasn't a laughing matter. Once Joe had made the connection between Noreen and her photographer, the trail had been easy to follow. Noreen and Ramon Gonzales hadn't tried to cover their tracks. It was just that no one except Chloe had known about that home pregnancy kit. It would have been one thing if Noreen had left Joe. How could she have left her daughter?

"I'm flying to Mexico in a few hours. You probably don't think that's wise."

"If you didn't kill her before, you won't now. I think what you're seeking is closure."

"My attorney and I are hand-delivering an affidavit and divorce papers. I want to get it over with."

"Chloe's welcome to stay here while you're gone, Joe."

He looked at her, took a step toward her, stopped. "If the press gets wind of it, and they will, it'll get ugly again. Since you live here now, your name will get dragged into it."

"Okay."

He did a double take. "That's all you have to say?"

There was a tingling in the pit of her stomach and a gentle warming elsewhere. "Chloe can stay with me and I'm not worried about the press. I handled it once and I can handle it again. Is that what you came to ask me?" She felt the ghost of a smile playing along the corners of her mouth. "Or is there something else?"

He crossed the grass. An instant later he had her in his arms. His mouth came down on hers, and the vibration in the pit of her stomach changed. She tilted her head as if they'd done this a million times.

This was what the universe had been telling her tonight. This was what she'd been waiting for, and so had Joe. He brought his hands to either side of her face, sliding his fingers into her hair, to her neck and shoulders, his touch persuasive and possessive, reckless and yet predestined.

Tomorrow, Lila would take the kiss apart and

analyze it with her friends, the way women often did. Katherine would say it was a kiss made of the kind of heat that soldered metal, and Pepper would insist that kisses like this were in the same league as shopping on Rodeo Drive. For Lila, it was a memory in the making.

The kiss ended in its own time, slowly, gently, sweetly, just as thunder rumbled in the distance. For some reason Lila thought of Myrtle Ann.

"Do you remember the first time we met?" she asked. "You told me the names of the goats and the rooster."

"You never told me your name that day," he asked.

"Didn't I?"

He shook his head.

And she said, "We've never been properly introduced. I'm Lila Delaney."

After a moment, he said, "And I'm Joe Schmoe."

"I'm pleased to make your acquaintance."

A gentle breeze blew and rain fell softly from the low, black sky. From somewhere came another soft rumble. It might have been thunder. It might have been someone dancing on the moon. Or it might have been the glorious unfolding of a divine master plan.

* * * * *

Please turn the page for an exciting preview of
LATE BLOOMERS *by Peggy Webb,*
available in February from Harlequin NEXT.

Emily

I feel like a hot-house tomato somebody jerked out of the pot and stuffed in the ground, then forgot to water.

I thought I was doing fine, all dressed up, finally back on the piano bench at Smithville Baptist Church playing the prelude.

Then Laura McCord, the town's failed opera singer and chief busybody, leaned over and said, "*Psst*, Emily. Your shoes."

Good Lord. One blue and one black. That's what I get for trying to be a Nancy Reagan kind of widow who glides gracefully through grief instead of what I am—a slightly hysterical, totally clueless, recently bereaved woman who doesn't have the foggiest idea how I'll get through the rest of my life without Mike Jones.

I don't think I should get out of the house again for about six years. Why didn't I take Delta's advice? She's smarter than I am, more educated, more beautiful, more *everything*. If she weren't my first cousin and best friend, I'd hate her.

"Emily, you've got to let yourself grieve. Hole up and just let it rip. Stop prancing around trying to act like Bob Hope entertaining the troops."

That's me to a T, always front and center, making sure everybody is having a good time, spinning tales, making them laugh. Even in the aftermath of death, for Pete's sake.

Delta writes travel guides at the speed of light—a workaholic, both her husbands said—and I finally convinced her to go to Hot Springs where she's researching not one but *two*—a guide to spas and a guide to great Southern restaurants.

Although I'm three years older, it has always seemed the reverse to me. She came into this world screeching and batting her fists against the injustice of being jerked out of the safe haven of the womb into a remorseless world.

I hugged her hard and then said, "You go on now, Delta. It's high time for me to grow up."

She knew exactly what I meant. Mike petted and pampered and protected me from life's messy chores such as balancing checkbooks. If I'm to survive without him, I've got to start learning how to do a few things by myself.

But first I have to finish playing the prelude. I don't

know what possessed me to think I could sit here only three months after the funeral praising the Lord with music instead of wanting to box his Holy jaws for prematurely jerking my husband up to Glory Land.

"*Psst*, Emily." Laura McCord taps me on the shoulder again. "Stop it. I don't believe this church is ready for rock-a-billy."

To my mortification I realize I've segued from high church music to Ray Charles's *Mess Around*.

Maybe I'm losing my mind and only imagining myself a widow. Maybe Mike is holed up somewhere right now consulting with the best psychiatrists about my care.

When I get home I hear the recorded message on my answering machine: "Hello. You've reached Mike and Emily Jones. We're not home right now, but please leave a message."

Well, he's half right. Emily's here, but Mike's not. Maybe that's him calling to say he'll be late driving back from wherever he is—Texas, to advise his bossy sister Lucille about the family ranch—and I should save him some pie.

But no, it's Delta.

"Emily, are you there? Pick up."

I grab the phone as if it's my lifeline. Which *it is*.

"I'm here," I say, and then I start bawling. Delta is the only person besides Mike I've allowed to see every one of my feelings and emotions, no matter how messy or ridiculous.

When my cat, Leo, became the victim of a hit-and-run because I was too busy being a newlywed to see him streaking through the open door, Mike got a new kitten for me. But Delta came over with a six-pack of Hershey's bars with almonds, two white candles for an all-night vigil and a book called *Cat Hymns* for the memorial service.

"Em, I'm coming right home, and don't try to stop me."

She had nothing to lose...

With a hurricane bearing down on New Orleans,
the failed nurse-turned-waitress viewed it as
an opportunity—to escape her tattered life.
It was time to rebuild—her life, her city—
on a foundation of hope.

Blink of an Eye

USA TODAY bestselling author
Rexanne Becnel

Available February 2007
TheNextNovel.com

HN77

It's never too late to take that flying leap

Two friends set off for the Tuscan countryside
to heal wounds of the past. Through the
strength of their friendship, both women
discover they can face the future and embrace
its limitless possibilities....

Late Bloomers

by

Peggy Webb

Available February 2007
TheNextNovel.com

HN78

This February...

Catch NASCAR Superstar **Carl Edwards** *in*

SPEED DATING!

Kendall assesses risk for a living—
so she's the last person you'd
expect to see on the arm of a
race-car driver who thrives on the
unpredictable. But when a bizarre
turn of events—and NASCAR
hotshot Dylan Hargreave—inspire
her to trade in her ever-so-structured
existence for "life in the fast lane"
she starts to feel she might be
on to something!

**Collect all 4 debut novels in
the Harlequin NASCAR series.**

SPEED DATING
by *USA TODAY* bestselling author
Nancy Warren

THUNDERSTRUCK
by Roxanne St. Claire

HEARTS UNDER CAUTION
by Gina Wilkins

DANGER ZONE
by Debra Webb

**On sale
February
2007**

www.eHarlequin.com   NASCARFEB

HARLEQUIN® *Romance*®

What a month!

In February watch for

Rancher and Protector

Part of the Western Weddings miniseries

BY JUDY CHRISTENBERRY

The Boss's Pregnancy Proposal

BY RAYE MORGAN

Also in February, expect
MORE of what you love
as the Harlequin Romance line
increases to six titles per month.

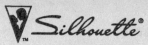

Romantic
SUSPENSE

Excitement, danger and passion guaranteed!

Same great authors and riveting editorial
you've come to know and love.

Look for our new name next month
as Silhouette Intimate Moments® becomes
Silhouette® Romantic Suspense.

Bestselling author
Marie Ferrarella
is back with a hot
new miniseries—
The Doctors Pulaski:
Medicine just got
more interesting....

Check out her
first title,
**HER LAWMAN
ON CALL,**
next month.

Look for it wherever
you buy books!

Visit Silhouette Books at www.eHarlequin.com   SIMRS0107

Silhouette

Desire

Don't miss the first book
in THE ROYALS trilogy:

THE FORBIDDEN PRINCESS
(SD #1780)

by national bestselling author

DAY LECLAIRE

Moments before her loveless royal wedding,
Princess Alyssa was kidnapped by a mysterious man
who'd do anything to stop the ceremony. Even if that
meant marrying the forbidden princess himself!

On sale February 2007 from Silhouette Desire!

THE ROYALS
Stories of scandals and secrets
amidst the most powerful palaces.

Make sure to read the other titles in the series:
THE PRINCE'S MISTRESS
On sale March 2007
THE ROYAL WEDDING NIGHT
On sale April 2007

*Available wherever books are sold, including most
bookstores, supermarkets, discount stores and drugstores.*

Visit Silhouette Books at www.eHarlequin.com   SDTFP0207

HARLEQUIN Presents

Welcome back to the exotic land of Zuran, a beautiful
romantic place where anything is possible.

**Experience a night of passion
under a desert moon in**

Arabian Nights

Spent at the sheikh's pleasure...

Drax, Sheikh of Dhurahn, must find a bride for his brother—
and who better than virginal Englishwoman Sadie Murray?
But while she's in his power, he'll test her wife-worthiness
at every opportunity....

TAKEN BY
THE SHEIKH
by Penny Jordan

Available this February.
Don't miss out on your chance to own it today!

www.eHarlequin.com

HPAN0207

REQUEST YOUR FREE BOOKS!

2 FREE NOVELS PLUS 2 FREE GIFTS!

There's the life you planned. And there's what comes next.

YES! Please send me 2 FREE Harlequin® NEXT™ novels and my 2 FREE mystery gifts. After receiving them, if I don't wish to receive any more books, I can return the shipping statement marked "cancel." If I don't cancel, I will receive 3 brand-new novels every month and be billed just $3.99 per book in the U.S., or $4.74 per book in Canada, plus 25¢ shipping and handling per book applicable taxes, if any*. That's a savings of over 20% off the cover price! I understand that accepting the 2 free books and gifts places me under no obligation to buy anything. I can always return a shipment and cancel at any time. Even if I never buy anything from Harlequin, the two free books and gifts are mine to keep forever.

156 HDN EF3R 356 HDN EF3S

Name _____ (PLEASE PRINT)

Address _____ Apt. #

City _____ State/Prov. _____ Zip/Postal Code

Signature (if under 18, a parent or guardian must sign)

Order online at www.TryNEXTNovels.com

Or mail to the **Harlequin Reader Service®:**

IN U.S.A.: P.O. Box 1867, Buffalo, NY 14240-1867
IN CANADA: P.O. Box 609, Fort Erie, Ontario L2A 5X3

Not valid to current Harlequin NEXT subscribers.

Want to try two free books from another line?
Call 1-800-873-8635 or visit www.morefreebooks.com

* Terms and prices subject to change without notice. NY residents add applicable sales tax. Canadian residents will be charged applicable provincial taxes and GST. This offer is limited to one order per household. All orders subject to approval. Credit or debit balances in a customer's account(s) may be offset by any other outstanding balance owed by or to the customer. Please allow 4 to 6 weeks for delivery.

Your Privacy: Harlequin is committed to protecting your privacy. Our Privacy Policy is available online at www.eHarlequin.com or upon request from the Reader Service. From time to time we make our lists of customers available to reputable firms who may have a product or service of interest to you. If you would prefer we not share your name and address, please check here. ☐

NEXT07